Book One in The JACK REACHER Cases

THE JACK REACHER CASES (A MAN MADE FOR KILLING)

DAN AMES

Copyright © 2017 by Dan Ames

Published by Slogan Books, Inc., New York, NY.

FREE BOOKS AND MORE

Would you like a FREE copy of my story BULLET RIVER?

Then sign up for the DAN AMES BOOK CLUB

AuthorDanAmes.com

A MAN MADE FOR KILLING

THE JACK REACHER CASES

BOOK #3

by

Dan Ames

**It is much more difficult to avoid wickedness,
for it runs faster than death.**

-Socrates

CHAPTER ONE

The body washed ashore in pieces. Each successive wave brought fresh evidence of a unique horror inflicted upon what was once a young woman.

When the tide receded, hours later as dawn began to break, the first of the gulls appeared overhead.

Simultaneously, a man emerged from the early morning fog. He ran with a slow purpose along the beach.

His name was Michael Tallon.

He was used to death.

He'd seen it in Iraq. Then again in Afghanistan. And in a few other places in the world he wasn't allowed to talk about.

Even here on San Clemente Island, a remote barrier island off the coast of California, he knew he wasn't immune to it. It was here that special forces personnel often spent a great deal of time. Sometimes they came here to train. Other times, it was their first stop back from duty overseas. They came here first because it was a safe place to begin the decompression process. Not safer for the special forces, safer for the people around them.

Still, even among professionals, accidents happened. And other things did, too, that weren't always accidents.

Running on San Clemente Island was not to be undertaken lightly. The island was quite large, nearly twenty-five miles long and five miles wide. It had been used as an artillery range by Navy ships for decades. Now, it was a place shared by many different groups of the military. Some who knew each other. Some who didn't.

And the public hardly knew about the place at all.

The ground was still full of ordnance, some of it unexploded.

Tallon was a pro and he had spent a lot of time on the island. He knew when and where to run.

One of those spots was along the Western coastline of the island. It was hard to get to and you could see where you were putting your feet.

So now, he turned up his pace as he neared the halfway point of his out-and-back run.

The morning sun was barely up and it was cold, yet sweat glistened on Tallon's forehead and his legs were slick.

San Clemente Island really didn't have a beach per se, simply larger outcroppings of rock with patches of sand here or there. This section of the island was the closest to being an actual beach and Tallon powered his way down the sand to the edge of the water.

As he slowed to a stop he noticed a large pile of sea cabbage, a frequent deposit found on the rocks. But a flash of white caught Tallon's eye and he went closer to the clump.

His breath slowed and he felt the warmth of the sun as it began to burn through the faint morning mist.

Tallon stopped.

He realized the small pile wasn't cabbage at all.

It was the shredded remains of a torso.

A female torso, as he recognized the sight of one breast that remained intact on the body.

He let out a long breath and looked around.

There was no one else here.

Tallon stepped closer to the remains and noted there were more deposited in a rough line along the remains of the outgoing tide.

He could make out chunks of human flesh. A severed limb that was most likely an arm.

Shark.

The island was surrounded by great white sharks, Tallon knew. You often saw them from the plane that brought personnel out from Los Angeles. Flying overhead you could frequently see the huge sharks, never swimming together, but on the prowl for the sea lions that made their home at various points along the shore.

The wounds on the torso were clear. Shredded skin that could only be a shark. He didn't know if it was a great white or not, but whatever it was had done its damage.

The rest was a mystery. There were no surfers out here. No one swam for recreation. Hell, even the Navy guys were careful about going in the water.

And then Tallon's breath caught in his throat.

Because he was looking at the foot that was partially covered with sand.

Peeking out of the sand was the top of a tattoo.

The ink on the skin was a rendering of a bird's wings.

Tallon let out the breath that he had been holding.

A chill went through his body.

He knew who she was.

CHAPTER TWO

"Jack Reacher needs your help."

Those were the words that had brought Pauling from New York to northern Wisconsin to meet with one of the wealthiest men in the country, Nathan Jones.

Now, Pauling drove her rental car, an SUV, up the long, winding drive to the sprawling log home that looked out over Barrel Lake. It was a private lake with only one home located on its shores.

It was a classic log home, but on a grander scale than most had ever imagined. It had a towering entrance with twin posts and a large steeped roof. There was an intricate carving above the front entrance, bigger than most double garages.

Pauling parked her vehicle on the circular drive, just past the entrance. Barrel Lake was reflected in the dozens of panoramic windows facing out from the house. A steady breeze blew in from the lake and in the distance, she saw a few whitecaps. The wind had picked up, and the fishing wouldn't be as good.

As Pauling walked to the front door she considered Nathan's call.

Her first thought was surprise that Jack Reacher needed help from her. More accurately, that Jack Reacher needed help, period.

Reacher was a guy who could handle anything on his own.

And most likely, had.

Still, Pauling was intrigued enough to meet with Nathan Jones. He had promised first-class accommodations and a week's worth of pay just to meet with him.

Pauling had done her research.

Nathan Jones had made a fortune in the paper business, the lumber business and the stock market, in that order. Not only did he own Barrel House, the name of his estate that referred to his love of blues music, but he had an apartment in Manhattan and a penthouse condo in the Florida Keys.

Pauling walked up to the deck that had sweeping views of the lake, and noticed her reflection in the huge bank of windows and sliding glass doors.

She was still in great shape. Over the years she'd had a lot of self-defense training and in addition to traditional work-outs, she frequently dropped in on martial arts classes to keep her reflexes sharp.

The woman looking back at her was in good shape, with light, blonde hair cut short but stylish, a lean face with startling green eyes hidden behind a pair of Ray Ban aviator sunglasses.

Pauling peeked inside the house through the sliding glass doors.

Nathan Jones stood in the great room, looking out toward the lake, with a glass of whiskey in his hand. He waved Pauling inside.

"Hello," she said.

"Lauren Pauling, thank you for coming on such short notice."

"Thank you for the invitation."

"Can I get you something to drink?"

"Sure," she said. "Whatever you're having."

He nodded and went to a sideboard where a decanter of whiskey and several glasses sat.

Pauling studied him as he poured her drink. Nathan was a big man, with broad shoulders and just a bit of gut beginning to hang over the edge of his pants. But he had a fine head of silver hair, ruddy cheeks, and the presence of a man who was used to getting things done. And getting them done his way.

Nathan returned with a drink in hand. He gave it to Pauling and then took a seat in one of the big chairs that flanked the main window looking out at the lake.

Pauling chose a chair across from him.

"So you said Jack Reacher needed help," Pauling said.

"Yes," Jones said. "I asked him to do a favor for me, and now he says he needs your help."

Pauling shook her head.

"Hard to believe, but I'll play along," she said. "What does he need help with?"

"It's about my daughter, Paige," Nathan said. "I'm sorry to be blunt, but she's dead."

"I'm sorry for your loss," Pauling said.

"What happened?" she asked.

"They say she drowned," Jones answered. He took a drink of liquor. "The story is she drowned and then sharks attacked her. Or vice versa."

His voice trembled briefly before he regained his composure. Pauling noted the sarcastic emphasis Jones had placed on the word *story*.

"She was working on San Clemente Island," he said. "Studying the Shrike. It's a kind of endangered bird."

"San Clemente?" Pauling thought the name sounded familiar but she couldn't place it.

"It's one of the Channel Islands off the coast of southern California. Owned by the Department of Defense."

"Was she working for the government?"

"No. That species of bird is endangered. Paige was working for the Bird Conservatory. They have a whole program out there to basically protect the bird population and try to get it to grow."

Pauling took a sip of Scotch. It wasn't her kind of drink, but it gave her a little time to think.

"When did this happen?" she asked.

"Six weeks ago."

Pauling straightened in her chair.

"Six weeks ago?"

"Yes. It took me awhile to determine the quality of the investigation."

"The police are investigating?"

"That's just it, they aren't."

Suddenly, Pauling was struck by where the conversation was going.

"I see," she started to say.

"It's all bullshit," Jones finally blurted out. He had seen the realization in her face.

"What's bullshit?"

"Everything the cops told me," Jones said.

"That she drowned?"

"Paige didn't drown," Jones said, his voice as harsh as sandpaper. He tossed down the rest of his Scotch and banged his glass down on the table next to his chair.

"She was murdered."

CHAPTER THREE

Pauling wasn't sure she had heard right. She figured
Nathan Jones was a pragmatic man. A mourning
parent often had the inability to think clearly.

Pauling chose her words carefully. She had seen more than
her fair share of death and killing. It was instinctive to believe
that accidents just can't happen – that a loved one can't be
dead just by a cruel twist of fate. It gave comfort, in an odd
way, for family members to believe that it had been a part of
someone's plan.

But she had her doubts about this one.

"Why do you say that?" she asked.

He held out his thick hands and grabbed his pointer
finger.

"One. Paige was not a swimmer. Not even close. The only
time she ever enjoyed getting in the ocean was in the
Caribbean," he said. "And even then, she liked to stay shallow
where she could see the bottom. When we went snorkeling
she absolutely did not want to go out into deeper water."

"I can see that," Pauling said.

"Hell, half the time when we were traveling she didn't

even want to swim in the goddamned hotel swimming pool. No way she would have gone out into that water. No way in hell," he said. His face was flushed and his voice had grown in both volume and intensity.

Pauling knew instinctively that what he was saying he unequivocally believed to be true.

"Two," Nathan continued. "We did some research. That water around San Clemente, at that time of year, is absolutely freezing. It's ice cold. There's just no way in hell Paige, who didn't like the water all that much to begin with, would suddenly decide to swim in fifty degree water. Absolutely no way in hell that was happening."

That made sense to Pauling. She'd spent more than her fair share of time in southern California. The water was usually pretty cold.

"And three, that water around the island is not conducive to swimming," Nathan concluded. "First of all, there are a ton of sea lions around the island so there are about a bazillion sharks. And not the little bitty ones like you see in Florida. I'm talking the big boys. Great whites. Even the Navy guys who train there don't like to swim. And two, the water isn't very clear. In some spots it might be. But in most, it's not. So you tell me, would a girl who doesn't like to swim suddenly decide to jump in water that's ice-cold, murky, and full of sharks?"

To avoid answering, Pauling took another drink of her Scotch.

"No," Nathan said. "Absolutely not."

"What if she had gone out on a boat? Fallen off the boat and then drowned?"

"Whose boat?" Nathan countered. "Why didn't they alert the authorities? I checked, there were no missing boats during that time period. No sailboats gone missing. Plus, Paige had been working on the island."

"So what do you think happened?" Pauling asked. Nathan Jones had already done a lot of thinking and researching.

He finished off his glass of liquor before speaking. "What I think is that someone killed her and dumped her body out in the ocean and then let the sharks destroy the evidence."

Nathan slammed his empty glass down onto the table next to his chair.

"In fact, that's not what I think happened. That's exactly what happened. I know it more than I've ever known anything in my life."

He pointed his thick finger at her.

"That's why I got in touch with Jack Reacher. And now I need you to go out there and help him."

Jones leaned forward, the intensity coming off him in waves.

"You and Jack Reacher need to find the bastard who killed my daughter."

CHAPTER FOUR

"Here's why you and Reacher are the perfect pair to get the bottom of what happened to my daughter," Nathan said.

Pauling figured Nathan Jones was a master of negotiation so she sat back and listened.

"First of all, you're highly intelligent." He smiled at her. "Top of your class. Every Ivy League school wanted you. Second, you have an impressive background with some experience dealing with the military. Reacher's resumé speaks for itself in that regard."

He looked out the window at the lake. An eagle flew low looking for a fish. It careened back upward. No sign of prey.

"You're the right gender as well," he said. "This place is about as male-dominated as you can get. If I only sent a man in there, it would become a bullshit testosterone macho contest. You can infiltrate much more effectively than some swinging dick like Reacher. The fact that you're beautiful will only help matters. The two of you will make a perfect tag-team."

To anyone else, it would have sounded sexist, but Pauling understood the man before her. His mind didn't work that way. He was all about strategy and aggression. Nothing more, nothing less.

"Reacher is already there, doing his thing. As far as your role, I've worked out an arrangement with the Bird Conservatory, thanks in part to their regret over what happened to my daughter," he said, his voice dripping with sarcasm. "It probably doesn't hurt either that I made a huge contribution to their fund awhile back."

Pauling sighed.

Nathan Jones was a force of nature.

He gestured toward the backpack and held up the envelope.

"Here's everything you'll need," he said. "A copy of the bullshit police report. Travel arrangements. Plane tickets. Dossiers on some of the individuals you'll meet. Phone numbers. Contact lists. Email addresses."

He put the envelope back into the pack.

"There's also a satellite phone, preprogrammed with my number and Blake Chandler's number. Blake is my computer guy."

Nathan Jones continued. "There's even a specially programmed laptop which has some uplink capabilities, courtesy of Blake. He'll be in touch with you if you need anything. There's also twenty grand in cash. Use it if you need it. And I will pay you for your time, double your normal fee. No matter how long it takes. Does that work for you?"

Pauling really hadn't planned on taking the case. She was overworked already. But the idea of working with Reacher again was too good to pass up.

"Yes," she replied.

"Great. Read through everything. We can fly you out there as soon as you're ready."

He got to his feet. Spoke softly, his voice trembling. "Find out who killed my girl."

CHAPTER FIVE

The tiny log cabin located on Acorn Lake was just a few miles from Nathan Jones's sizeable domain. The cabin had been rented for her, just for the meeting with Nathan Jones.

Now, Pauling pulled the Land Rover into the gravel driveway, parked, got out and unlocked the cabin's front door. She walked inside and set the backpack Nathan had given her down on the couch.

The cabin consisted of one room that contained an open kitchen, a living area with a wood burning fireplace, a small dining table, and a loft with a bed. The only other room was the bathroom just off of the kitchen. The walls were knotty pine. The giant picture window facing the lake provided all of the cabin's decoration.

Pauling went to the refrigerator and pulled out a bottle of Chardonnay. She poured herself a glass, dug out the envelope from the backpack and walked out onto the cabin's front porch. Two weathered Adirondack chairs sat facing the lake. She took the one nearest the door, sat down and set the folder in her lap.

She took a drink of wine and studied Acorn Lake.

It was much smaller than Barrel Lake. The water wasn't as clear and there were more widespread weed beds. Trees towered along the lake, dropping their acorns into the water, giving the lake its name. They also caused the water to turn darker.

It was hard not to feel compassion for Nathan Jones and a a wave of sadness for his daughter.

She also felt an eagerness and excitement to see Reacher again. Had he changed? What was going on that he needed her help? And did he really need her help or did he just want to see her again?

As she gazed out at the lake, saw the sky turning from blue to dark red at its edges, she thought about the situation.

Pauling looked down at the envelope in her lap, opened it and pulled out the thick sheaf of papers.

The travel documents were first, with airplane tickets and a hotel reservation in Los Angeles. She glanced at the dates. Yes indeed, he wanted her leaving as soon as possible.

Pauling put the travel papers back in the envelope.

Next, she skimmed the contact list and the instructions for using both the sat phone and the laptop.

The dossiers she didn't even glance at. Those she could read later.

The police report was only two pages long. A clear case of drowning. It appeared as if no other detective work had been attempted.

Finally, she pulled out a leather journal. When she opened it, a photograph fell out. A note was attached that told her it was Paige Jones, a year ago, standing at the top of an old wooden tower that had been built to look out over a sinkhole in the state forest a dozen or so miles from Barrel Lake.

Paige had been a beautiful girl. Dark hair, startling blue eyes, and an enigmatic smile.

She opened the journal and saw another note. It was Paige's journal.

It wasn't a diary, but rather notes from the field on habitat and wildlife. There was no date on either inside cover.

Pauling put the journal back in the envelope and studied the mirrored surface of the lake.

The sun was setting, and a tangerine sky was now sporting subtle shades of purple. It would disappear behind the trees in less than a half hour.

Pauling gently nudged backward and the sound of the rocking chair creaking on the wooden porch seemed obscenely loud.

Another eagle, maybe the same one from Barrel Lake, appeared over the treetops and dove toward the surface of the water.

This time, it dove sharply and its claws tore through the water.

When it surged upward, it had a fish in its talons.

It reminded her of Jack Reacher, and a saying her old boss often used.

A true hunter never stops hunting.

CHAPTER SIX

I t was early morning, before school, when her Dad gave her a big hug and a kiss. He was going on another one of his business trips. This time, it was to New York. He'd been there before. The last time he'd gone he'd come back with a snow globe that had a miniature Statue of Liberty inside.

Pauling had put it on her little desk in her room.

The next day, she was at school when the teachers began acting strangely.

Classes were stopped. Teachers whispered to one another.

They let the kids out early and Pauling practically skipped home.

But when she saw her Mom she knew something was wrong.

Tears were streaming down her face.

The television was on in the living room.

Pauling's father had died in the 9/11 attack on the World Trade Center.

And later, when she was in college at the top of her class with a stellar command of languages and saw that an FBI agent was coming to campus, she thought of that day.

Not long after, she went to the campus library and read every book she could get her hands on about the FBI. Even though the CIA *was primarily leading the charge on terrorism overseas, the FBI took care of domestic issues. For Pauling, the FBI held great appeal.*

So she studied everything she could about the FBI. She read the good books and she read the bad books.

Eventually she picked up the phone and made the call.

And after a short two-week vacation upon graduation from college, she joined the FBI.

CHAPTER SEVEN

She wasn't surprised to receive a call from Nathan Jones. He'd probably made a large part of his fortune by being able to read people. And as good as Pauling's poker face was, when she'd learned that Reacher needed her help, she was already in.

"Blake will pick you up at six a.m. sharp," Nathan said. "Plenty of time since your flight doesn't leave until nine-thirty. He'll return your rental car later."

Pauling had glanced at the itinerary and knew that from the small airport in northern Wisconsin she would fly to Milwaukee and then from there to Los Angeles.

"I have to be honest with you," Pauling explained. "I don't feel there's a high probability of success on this."

His response was immediate. "Something like this you don't play the odds," he said. "You make them. I have a sense of how you like to work, Pauling, and my guess is it's a lot like mine."

Pauling wasn't so sure of that herself, but she had to admit that Nathan Jones was no doubt a highly driven person. And she'd been labeled with that term from time to time herself.

"Every wall you run into you see as a temporary obstruction," Nathan continued. "Your first instinct is to go right through it. If that doesn't work, you find a way around. But then you go back and remove it anyway, just in case you have to come back that way."

Pauling smiled at the compliment. It made a sort of sense to her and it was a statement she couldn't disagree with.

"Walls and bridges, sometimes they have to be destroyed," she said.

"Now you're really sounding like me," Nathan said with no small amount of satisfaction. "Good luck and stay in touch. Make your first progress report whenever you feel like you have something you want to share. This is your show, not mine."

It was her hope to find out everything she could within two weeks at the most. If she hadn't learned anything by then, Pauling figured spending even more time there wouldn't accomplish much.

At least, that was her goal. Maybe she could do it in two days and be back.

A lot of it depended on Jack Reacher.

A light rain had begun to make its way across the lake and now it was pattering against the cabin walls. Pauling built a fire in the fireplace, the last one she would probably enjoy for awhile and sat down on the couch.

Suddenly, she had an intense desire to talk to someone. Anyone. Pauling looked at her phone. There were a few people she could call, including her sister, but she decided against it.

Instead, Pauling dug out Paige's journal from the backpack and opened it.

She read through the first few pages which consisted of notes regarding ground cover and a bunch of long, complicated names in Latin. Maybe once she was on the island she could talk to someone who would be able to interpret for her.

On the fourth page, there was a beautiful drawing of a bird. It was perched on a thorny branch. Next to it, there was the body of a mouse.

The mouse had been impaled on one of the tree's thorns.

Beneath the drawing, Paige had written three words.

The Butcher Bird.

CHAPTER EIGHT

In the morning, Blake arrived and Pauling threw her things into the SUV. She climbed into the passenger seat.

"I grabbed you a coffee," he said. "Black, right?"

"Thanks, yes," she said. "Where did you get it? Isn't the nearest Starbucks about a hundred miles away?"

"I picked it up at the mini-mart at the edge of town. It's not great, but not bad, either. I was going to get you some jerky too and maybe a baseball cap with a drawing of a hunter standing over a deer with the caption *the buck stops here*."

Pauling blew on the coffee and took a sip. Not bad. Nice and strong the way she liked it.

Blake pulled out onto the dirt road, eventually making it to the rural highway where he was able to notch the speed up significantly.

"By the way, I meant to compliment you on your poker face," Pauling said. "We fished together all day and you never once mentioned Nathan's plan."

A sheepish expression came across Blake's face. "Honestly, I didn't know his plan and he didn't really tell me. It was more of a technical request. But once he started asking me to do specific things with documents, phone numbers, addresses and email addresses I started to guess it was going to involve you."

"I'm just giving you shit, Blake." She felt bad making him explain himself.

"Oh," he said, looking relieved. "You know Nathan. No one wants to get on his bad side."

There was an awkward silence between them.

"You're not asking where I'm going and what I'm doing because you don't want to know, right?" she guessed.

Blake drummed his thin, pale fingers on the steering wheel. Pauling guessed he'd been spending a lot more time in his office on the computers than in the boat fishing.

"It wouldn't take a genius to guess it has something to do with Paige. But exactly what you're doing and how you're going to get involved in it, well–"

"Do you want to know?"

"You tell me," he answered. "I don't want to know if I'm not *supposed* to know."

"Okay," Pauling said. "To put an end to this goofy conversation, I'm going to say it's on a need-to-know basis and right now, you don't need to know exactly what I'm doing. But I believe you're going to be a resource for me. Did Nathan at least explain that?"

"Yeah, he kind of mentioned it. Again, in a general sense."

"Okay, we're in agreement then," Pauling said. "Although depending on what I find, the level of your involvement could change quickly. How's that?"

"Fine with me," Blake said. "I've been in the dark most of my life. I like it there."

Pauling laughed. She loved Blake and how self-deprecating he always was. It was refreshing from the host of alpha males she had always been forced to deal with.

They talked a lot about former high school friends and what they were doing as the rain abated and a few tentative shafts of sunlight appeared in the horizon. The landscape changed from thick trees to gently rolling hills and eventually they found the airport.

It was a single building with a few parked cars in front. Behind the building, they could see the runway and an airplane that appeared to be idling.

"I think that's Nathan's private plane," Blake said.

Pauling got out of the Explorer and hoisted her backpack onto her shoulder. Blake retrieved the one rolling suitcase she was bringing.

That was it.

"Be careful," Blake said.

"I'll shoot first and ask questions later."

Blake hugged her.

"I would expect nothing less."

CHAPTER NINE

The flight was going to be so short Pauling didn't bother breaking open her backpack to do any more investigating. Nathan's private plane was going to take her to Milwaukee, and from there, she would catch a commercial flight to Los Angeles.

So she simply enjoyed the scenery on the small plane, felt some of the despondency that had begun to sink in now fall away as the aircraft lifted off.

Beneath her, Wisconsin's green rolling hills flattened out into traditional quadrants of farm fields. Occasionally, a stand of trees had been planted to serve as windbreaks.

It seemed they had barely leveled off before the pilot announced they were beginning their descent.

The plane touched down and she was escorted across the tarmac and back into a terminal where a commercial flight was boarding for Los Angeles.

She took a quick detour to get a bottle of water and a bag of nut mix.

Pauling preferred to stand while waiting for the plane to

board and soon she was in the first-class line and then promptly showed her seat.

No one sat next to her and the fight attendant asked her if she wanted a drink. She was about to say no, then changed her mind and asked for a Bloody Mary. Why not?

Eventually, the boarding doors closed with first class still half-empty, even after the few upgrades had taken place. The seat next to Pauling was still empty and she moved her backpack from the foot space in front of her and plopped it into the seat next to her.

Pauling sipped her Bloody Mary, which tasted surprisingly good and closed her eyes. She thought about trying to sleep but she was too well-rested.

Pauling opened the backpack, pushed aside Paige's journal and instead took out the file with background information on San Clemente Island. Whatever researcher Nathan had hired to provide background for her had done a very good job. The information was presented in a very neat and orderly fashion.

San Clemente Island sat sixty-eight miles off the coast of California and was part of the Channel Islands. It was twenty-one miles long and nearly five miles wide.

Native American remains dated to at least ten thousand years ago, and the island had been named by a Spanish explorer who'd discovered it on Saint Clement's Feast Day, hence San Clemente.

The United States military acquired the island in the 1930s, mainly as a ship-to-shore firing range. Training continued on the island to this day.

Tell me about the birds, Pauling thought as she skimmed through more of the island's vital statistics.

Finally, she got to the part she'd been looking for.

In the midst of the biggest live firing range the military owned, an endangered bird lived. The Shrike of San

Clemente. At one point, it had become one of the rarest birds in the world with only fourteen living individuals left.

When it was put on the endangered species list, the Bird Conservatory among others rushed in and began efforts to protect it. The military was immediately forced to cease some of its more "disruptive" activities and now worked in tandem with the naturalists to protect the bird.

Probably after some bad public relations, Pauling figured.

She read the last page and slipped the papers back into their folder and the folder went into the backpack.

She closed her eyes.

Imagine that. A rare bird in the middle of a live firing range on an island populated by what sounded like plenty of Special Operations soldiers.

And right in among all of that?

Paige Jones.

Beautiful.

Intelligent.

And apparently vulnerable.

Despite her conviction that dozing was not an option, Pauling began to drift off to sleep.

Had Paige Jones met Jack Reacher? If so, how had this happened? Pauling figured that Reacher had arrived after the murder.

Maybe because *of* it.

One final thought entered Pauling's mind.

She wondered if Paige Jones ever had any inkling of the dangers surrounding her on San Clemente Island.

In Pauling's sleep, no answer came.

CHAPTER TEN

It was a smooth landing but Pauling was wide awake before the rubber hit the road. They taxied into their parking spot and soon she was off the plane, through the terminal and when she descended via the escalator, she caught sight of a driver holding up a card emblazoned with her name.

Pauling almost laughed. When Nathan Jones arranged your travel, no expense was spared.

She approached the man holding the placard bearing her name, showed her identification and he took her out to a black Cadillac Escalade.

Fresh from the terminal, she stepped out into the southern California air and smiled. It was so much warmer and less humid than back in Wisconsin.

She climbed into the back while the driver put away her bags.

"From one airport to another," the driver said. He smiled at her from the rearview mirror.

"No rest for the wicked," Pauling answered.

He put the big SUV into gear and they wound their way

out of the airport before merging onto Sepulveda. They were heading south and Pauling knew from what Nathan had given her that the airport she would be going to wasn't exactly official. There were a number of planes and pilots that were pre-approved by the military people on San Clemente. It wasn't possible to get there without permission in the first place. Every plane had to have its manifest approved by the authorities on San Clemente Island.

Nathan had strategized that the best way forward was to have her listed as an employee of San Diego State who was volunteering her time with the Bird Conservatory. If anyone wished to take the time to run her identity, it would show the cover story Nathan had concocted; that she was an IT specialist. More of a general troubleshooter, really. That distinction would help her avoid anything too technical should an issue arise.

The good news, and the reason Nathan had chosen that role was that Pauling had learned quite a bit about computers, and had spent the majority of her workday on one at the FBI.

But she was not an IT specialist by any means.

She didn't really expect to have to defend her cover story that much anyway. She had gotten the sense that the bird people were constantly in the field while her story was that she would be checking and updating the main computer system in their office. And she could be vague enough about geeky computer code stuff to bore anyone to tears.

They headed south and Pauling soon recognized the area south of Los Angeles. Manhattan Beach. Long Beach. The sight of industrial areas and loading docks.

It was the part of Los Angeles tourists never saw and pictures of which never graced the front of postcards sent to the old folks back home.

They made their way past strip malls and the occasional

factory, with quick glimpses of tiny residential neighborhoods choked with parked cars packed tightly on the street bumper to bumper. Here and there groups of men stood on street corners and the occasional shopkeeper sweeping the walk in front of an ethnic grocery store.

The driver turned onto a street that looked more to Pauling like an alley than an actual traffic lane, eventually arriving at an impressive gate topped with razor wire. The driver said something into the intercom and the sturdy gate, sporting wheels on the bottom, rolled apart and the driver pulled the SUV ahead to an open aircraft hangar. He parked, helped Pauling with her bag and thanked her when she slipped him a twenty.

Hell, she had twenty grand in cash. The least she could do was be a good tipper.

Once the Escalade drove away, Pauling went into the open hangar.

There was a man with a clipboard and a walkie talkie on his hip. He was probably in his late thirties or early forties, brown hair with a touch of gray at the temples. He had on cargo pants and a jacket that was military green.

Behind him was a vintage airplane on display. Pauling wondered if it was one of the original Pan Am airplanes that were pre-WWII.

She was glad it appeared to be open to visitors.

She approached the man with the clipboard.

He looked up.

"Lauren Pauling?" he said.

"Hello."

He stuck out his hand. "Josh Troyer," he said. "I'm the flight coordinator for NASSCI."

A puzzled expression on Pauling's face made him chuckle.

"Naval Air Station San Clemente Island," he said. "We're really fond of acronyms around here."

"Got it," she said. Government speak was nothing new to her.

"You've got about twenty minutes if you want to grab a coffee or something," he said. "Facilities are over there." He pointed to public restrooms as well as a set of vending machines.

"Okay," Pauling said. "Is that exhibit open for viewing?" she said, pointing to the ancient plane. "I'd love to get a glimpse inside."

"Sure," he said. "An original DC-3. Built in 1930 or so. Yes, you can see the inside. After all, it's what you'll be flying in out to the island."

CHAPTER ELEVEN

They carefully weighed and stowed Pauling's gear and showed the same care for everything else that went onto the plane. Apparently they needed to be meticulous when it came to loading the old aircraft.

Troyer introduced her to the pilot, a man named Brock Jamison. He looked to be a little younger than Troyer. Slim, with dark hair and intense blue eyes. When he smiled, his teeth were jagged and crooked, ruining what would have been a strikingly handsome man. Pauling guessed he was a civilian pilot otherwise the military's dental plan would have taken care of those teeth.

"Hope you're not used to flying first class," Jamison said. She noticed that he actively worked to hide his teeth. He smiled only with his lips and at times it looked more like a grimace.

"No divas here," Pauling said. "How long is the flight?"

"Little over an hour, depending on wind," Jamison said. "Plus, top speed isn't very fast." He gestured at the plane behind them. "But she'll get us there. Hopefully."

Troyer made a sign of the cross and then both he and

Jamison chuckled. It looked like a little comedy routine.

It turned out, they were just getting started.

Pauling boarded the aircraft with the other passengers.

The interior was something else. It had been done up almost as some kind of Las Vegas lounge act. Velvet seats, velvet curtains over the windows, and purple carpet. The lights along the row between the seats were done in rainbow colors and there was rock music playing in the background.

All this airplane needs is a stripper pole, Pauling thought.

As the other passengers boarded, she tried to figure out who they were by their appearances, but it wasn't easy.

The military people were obvious, of course. She saw two people in Navy Seabee uniforms, one man and one woman. If Pauling recalled correctly the Seabees were the construction arm of the Navy.

There were two men wearing ties who looked like engineers. They had already broken out their laptops and appeared to be going over spreadsheets.

An entire group boarded the plane but Pauling had no idea who or what they might be. It was mostly guys, dressed in tan camo pants and Nike t-shirts. There was a woman, also dressed more in athletic gear than military gear.

Once everybody had found a seat, and nearly every seat was taken, the plane began to taxi toward the runway.

Troyer appeared from the cockpit, pushing a small cart. On its surface were bottles of beer along with an ice bucket in which a bottle of white wine had been placed.

"May I interest anyone in a beverage?" he said. The passengers erupted in applause. Pauling laughed and took a beer, just to join in.

As Troyer made the rounds, Jamison appeared, which made Pauling wonder, who exactly was in control of the plane?

"As some of you may or may not know, San Clemente

Island is one of the Channel Islands and home to a very robust population of sea lions." He had a martini glass in his hand and gestured with it as he spoke.

Pauling continued to look out the window as the plane flew, wondering exactly when autopilot had been invented and hoped that it was after the manufacture date of the aircraft. That, or maybe one had been retrofitted.

Either way, she hoped someone was paying attention.

"The sea lion's main predator is a teeny weeny fish called the great white shark," Jamison continued. He sipped from his martini and pulled out the olive and chomped it down.

"They literally surround San Clemente Island and attack anything in the water within a few feet of them," he said. He tossed down the rest of his martini and Pauling hoped that his title of "pilot" was ceremonious at best and there was really someone else who would fly the plane.

"With that in mind, today's entertainment on the short flight out to the island is a little film made by my good friend Steven Spielberg," Jamison continued. "It really made his reputation as a filmmaker and most of all, accurately captures the dangers surrounding San Clemente Island, especially if this old gal doesn't quite make it." He patted the ceiling above him.

"Enjoy the flight, folks!" he said and beamed at the passengers who half-heartedly raised their drinks in a mock toast.

Jamison disappeared behind the curtains that blocked the view to the cockpit, and Troyer returned the cart (now empty) to a spot just in front of the first row. He locked it in place and then joined Jamison at the helm.

On the video screens spaced periodically above the seats, the opening of the movie JAWS began to play.

Pauling smirked and drank her beer.

Well, she thought, *it was a great film.*

CHAPTER TWELVE

The shark on the screen was not alone.

As they approached the island, Pauling saw a huge, dark shadow languidly cruising less than a quarter mile from the island.

As if reading her mind, Jamison's voice spoke over the intercom.

"There's one of our native San Clementians as we speak."

Everyone found a window and watched the huge shark cruise its patrol.

Pauling couldn't help but think of Paige, and wondered if this was the same shark that may have gotten to her. All of the humor and jocularity of the flight instantly disappeared.

She drew the curtain on her window closed and thought about the job ahead.

There wasn't much to her cover. An IT specialist. Helping the bird people.

It could be done.

The descent was loud, slow and jarring. When they landed, it seemed like they went on forever, but Pauling knew the runway was actually very short. And she had read that the flight conditions themselves were very dangerous. High winds. Short runway. Small margin of error. Despite their bad comedy show, Pauling figured that Jamison and Troyer were probably very good at what they did.

Eventually the plane came to a stop and they disembarked. A young man in military clothing unloaded the gear and had it waiting for them on the tarmac. Although 'tarmac' was far too grandiose a word. The runway was cracked asphalt and another metal shed served as the airport's headquarters.

Pauling found her bags and carried them into the metal shed.

It reminded her vaguely of the small airport in northern Wisconsin, but this one was even more rustic. The vending machines were older. The floor was dirtier. And the smell was, well, *stronger*.

"Pauling?" a male voice said behind her.

She turned to find a curly-haired man, brushed with gray, wearing wire-rim glasses, a thick barn coat, blue jeans and Sperry boat shoes.

"Yes?" she said.

"My name is Dr. Abner Sirrine."

Pauling shook his hand, noting the soft grip. He made no move to help her with her bags. She thought he looked nervous.

"I'm parked right outside."

He turned and Pauling followed him to a filthy, older model Jeep Cherokee. It was white underneath a layer of dirt and grime.

Dr. Sirrine got behind the wheel.

Pauling loaded her bags into the backseat and then climbed into the front passenger space. The interior of the jeep was just as dirty as the outside. Gum wrappers, chunks of mud and grass, an empty Diet Coke can.

"So I guess I'll take you back to our HQ."

His voice was soft and tentative. She thought he sounded like a college professor or a high school biology teacher.

"Actually, can you give me a quick tour of the island?" Pauling asked. "Just to help me get my bearings."

She smiled at Dr. Sirrine and thought he seemed to relax a bit. In that moment, she understood why he was nervous. As always, she weighed the pros and cons of alleviating the tension. Sometimes it worked in your favor. For now, she decided to help him out.

"What were you told about the work I would be doing while I'm on the island?" she asked.

He gave her a look that was a cross between guilt and panic. "Well, no one would tell me exactly. Something about computer systems which is kind of odd because ours is really old and basic. Not much to analyze, really."

Nathan had told her she would be given a solid cover and she hadn't been on the island for more than a few minutes and someone was calling bullshit. Not a great start.

"That's part of it," Pauling said. "To study what you have and possibly make some recommendations on how to upgrade it or scrap it altogether and get something new."

"I see."

"And it's not just computers. My role is really to analyze the technology you're employing and prepare a report on how things can be improved and made more efficient. That's why I'll be involved in all aspects of what you're doing out here."

She thought he was going to protest so she quickly added, "Just as an observer, though. I'm not a biologist so I'll just try to stay out of your way."

This was also Pauling's way of letting him know that she would be needing to talk to everyone. From top to bottom.

"So what can you tell me about the island, Dr. Sirrine?" Pauling asked.

She'd already done her homework, but she got the sense that this was the kind of man who liked to hear himself talk, especially when it came to educating someone. Perhaps a female was also an inspiration.

"Fascinating history, really," Dr. Sirrine said.

Pauling chuckled silently.

Bingo.

CHAPTER THIRTEEN

"The earliest remains are from nearly ten thousand years ago. Most scholars believe it was the Tongva Native Americans with some influence from the Chumash as well."

They rounded a sharp curve and Pauling braced herself. Maybe it wasn't such a good idea to distract Dr. Sirrine. His driving skills couldn't afford it.

"From there the next stage was the Spanish conquest. A man named Juan Rodriguez Cabrillo discovered the island but it was named by a later explorer, Sebastian Vizcaino, who arrived on the island on the Feast of St. Clements Day. Hence the name."

"They must not have stayed around very long," Pauling said. "They didn't build anything. Not even a church?"

Dr. Sirrine shook his head. "No, the island is too far from the mainland."

Pauling watched a seagull fly over the jeep and in the distance, she saw a military helicopter.

"The most fascinating part of the history of the island

though isn't the people, it's the animals," Dr. Sirrine continued. "Although, I admit I'm probably not terribly objective."

Pauling was listening but she was stunned by the scenery. It was nearly apocalyptic. Very little shrubbery. Dirt roads that seemed to disappear over the edge of a cliff. Just bare land, the ocean in the background and sky. Fascinating. And surreal. She realized she'd never seen a place like this before. Anywhere.

"Feral animals, to be more specific," Dr. Sirrine continued. "It seems that some of the early peoples, or settlers after the Spanish, had goats. And when they left, a few of the goats remained. And naturally, the animals did what animals do. They ate and they reproduced. And ate some more and reproduced a lot more. At some point there were ten thousand goats on the island and not a stitch of green. No grass. No shrubs. No trees. Nothing."

It made sense to Pauling. To her, it looked like the landscape hadn't really recovered. The whole place felt like a Mad Max movie setting, on an island in the middle of the Pacific.

"So when the military bought the island, they had to get rid of the goats." Sirrine smiled and waggled a finger in the general direction of the windshield. He was really loosening up now. "They didn't kill them. Oh no, the public found out somehow and caused a huge uproar. So they had to airlift them off the island!" He laughed. "Can you believe it?"

"Operation Goat Removal," Pauling said.

"Yes! How bizarre!" Dr. Sirrine said. "And that's the whole story of why I'm out here. But there's plenty of time to tell you about that." His voice had taken on an edge of mystery.

"Habitat destruction?" Pauling said. "That's what led to the decline of all animal populations, right?"

Dr. Sirrine's eyes widened behind his glasses. "Yes, exactly. You've done your homework."

He sounded impressed and disappointed that he had been denied the answer to his mystery.

"I always took my homework seriously," Pauling said. Which was total bullshit. She had rarely done her homework when she was a student, preferring the all-night cram sessions fueled by pressure. It had been a game to her. It was only when she'd gotten a real job that she finally realized the need for daily focus.

"So now we're approaching the south end of the island?" she asked.

"Yes, this is where you'll be doing some fieldwork with the team. That is, if you really want to understand what we do."

"Yes, I do."

They drove in silence for several miles. Pauling was astounded continuously by what she saw. The landscape was like a huge tract of ocean front real estate that had yet to be discovered by the hotel people.

She could picture a Four Seasons Resort springing up or a tropical resort every mile or so. They would import tons of royal palm trees. They would have to make the island look lush and fertile, in a commercial sense. And that could certainly be accomplished, with a big enough landscaping budget.

But none of that would happen, after all, because the island was owned by the military. Pauling knew that the U.S. government was the biggest single owner of real estate in the country.

Dr. Sirrine continued to drive and Pauling was aware that he performed the task much better when he wasn't talking. However, she was here to gather information.

"So how many people are on your team?"

"Well, the number is fluid. People are constantly coming in and out of here due to the nature of their careers. We have some summer grad students, people on fellowships, volunteer observers and students who are only available for a semester or two. So there is actually a very high turnover, although we do everything we can to maintain some kind of continuity."

It was not what Pauling wanted to hear. She had hoped there would be more of a locked-room type of situation, so she could narrow the investigation as quickly as possible. But if people were coming and going on a regular basis it would make her job more difficult.

"Have you been working with Jack Reacher at all?" Pauling asked.

Dr. Sirrine looked at her. "Who?"

Pauling shook her head in reply.

"I'm going to turn here," Dr. Sirrine said. It was a strange little intersection. A sign to the right said RESTRICTED and there was a gate across the road. Although, with four-wheel drive, it seemed it would be relatively easy to drive around it.

"There are quite a few of those around." He glanced at her. "They don't look like much, but you have to pay attention to what they're saying. There are people with guns and live ammunition everywhere. If a sign says not to enter, take their advice and don't enter."

They continued on as the sun began to set. The ocean looked beautiful in the dying light.

"Is every sunset as spectacular as this?" Pauling said.

Dr. Sirrine looked up and out at the water.

"You know, I never really noticed."

CHAPTER FOURTEEN

T he road wound off to the side where a collection of buildings sat on a small rise. They were a combination of cinder block and aluminum. The main building had a row of parking spots in front of it. It was the cinder block building.

Above the main entrance was a wooden sign with the words THE NEST burned in by hand.

Dr. Sirrine pulled into the first parking spot next to the main building, and shut off the jeep.

"Welcome to The Nest as we call it," he said. He held up his hands. "Don't shoot me for the bad pun. Someone long before me came up with it."

"I like it," Pauling said.

"Bring your stuff in here and we'll figure out where you're staying," he said.

He went to the back of the jeep and grabbed his gear which consisted of a battered, brown leather backpack.

Pauling brought her gear through the door that Dr. Sirrine held open for her.

The space was one large room. Off to the left, a full

kitchen with a counter and a refrigerator and a few tables surrounded by plastic chairs.

The floor was industrial tile, plain white. The walls were standard beige and the ceiling was a classic dropped number that looked like it had come from an elementary school from the 1970s.

Directly ahead was a small living-room type area with a couch, love seat, and some mismatched chairs facing a large screen television that had been directly mounted to the wall.

Off to the right was a doorway that led to a hall.

Dr. Sirrine led her down the hallway where there were rooms spaced at lengthy intervals, with dark wood fiber doors that seemed more appropriate in a shoddily built office building.

The same tile floor was in place, and the hall smelled vaguely of disinfectant.

They came to the end of the hallway and one door remained.

"Ah yes, here you go," he said.

He used a key to open the door and then he flicked the light on inside and handed the key to Pauling.

"Home sweet home," he said.

Pauling stepped past him into the room. There was a dresser with a mirror above it. The dresser was made of flimsy particle board and it seemed to sag crookedly against the wall like it was too tired to hold up the mirror any longer.

There was a bed with a steel frame and no headboard. A mattress was on top of visible coiled springs and a stack of sheets and blankets were on top of the mattress.

A tiny bathroom was on the opposite side of the room.

There was a closet built into the wall across from the bed that looked like it could hold a half dozen t-shirts and not much else.

And next to the dresser was a desk that must have been

rescued from a middle school that was about to be demolished.

"Well, someone will probably be throwing together some kind of meal in the next hour or so," Dr. Sirrine said. "If you want to settle in and then come on up to the main room you can feel free. Nothing formal happens. But I think when someone is joining us, there is usually a meal."

"Okay, thank you. I will," Pauling said.

Dr. Sirrine backed out of the room and she could hear his footsteps down the hall.

Pauling unpacked, which took no time at all. She stuffed most everything into the shoddy drawers of the dresser, and hung a few things up in the tiny closet with a single bar.

At least the room was spotless. Someone had thoroughly cleaned the place since its last inhabitant. Pauling suddenly wondered if this had been Paige's room. She made a mental note to ask.

Finally, she unpacked the laptop, phone and all of the chargers and power cords that she would need and placed them all on the desk. There was an outlet just behind the desk and Pauling was glad she had thrown in a power strip. She plugged everything in.

Lastly, she took Paige's journal out of her backpack and tossed it onto the bed. She would read it before she went to sleep tonight.

One last stop into the bathroom where she splashed water on her face and then she closed the door, locking it behind her.

It was time to meet everyone.

And hopefully find Jack Reacher.

CHAPTER FIFTEEN

Pauling smelled the food first. She thought she detected onions, peppers and maybe a dash of cumin. If she had to guess, she would predict tacos were going to be the main course at tonight's dinner. Mexican food, for sure.

She came around the corner and saw a woman with dark hair, black glasses and a gray t-shirt standing over a large frying pan. The woman looked up at her.

"Hi," she said and smiled, revealing a row of teeth, tinged slightly red by the glass of wine next to her on the counter.

"Hello," Pauling responded. "Smells good."

"My standard chicken fajitas," the woman said. "If you see me cooking, odds are that nine out of ten times I'll be making fajitas. Kind of a one-hit wonder."

The woman put down the wooden spatula she had been using to stir the contents of the frying pan and stepped out from behind the counter. She thrust her hand out toward Pauling.

"I'm Janey Morris," she said. She was a small woman with pale skin and had the look of a nerdy librarian.

"Nice to meet you, I'm Pauling."

Janey smiled. "Abner said you'd be arriving today. How was the flight in?" Janey moved back to the pan and started to stir around the fajita ingredients.

Pauling looked around for a bottle of wine but didn't see one. She wouldn't mind a cocktail right about now, she thought.

Pauling noticed a second pan with a few tortillas warming.

"The flight was interesting," Pauling said. "I thought the plane was an antique for display purposes only. Didn't realize I'd actually be flying in it."

"I did the same thing," Janey said. "It was kind of cool. I felt like I was in an old Humphrey Bogart movie. And the guys are so funny. It was a really cool experience."

"They're funny the first time, but the routine gets old," a voice said from the living area. Pauling turned, realized she hadn't noticed the person sitting on the couch.

He was tall and thin with a face that sported an enormous jaw and big ears.

"Pauling, this is Ted. Ted, this is Pauling," Janey said, making the introductions.

Ted put down the book he had been reading, came over and shook Pauling's hand. Probably the kind of kid who was told by everyone to play basketball but was terribly uncoordinated. It was a hunch, but Pauling figured Ted wasn't very athletic.

"Want a beer?" he said.

"Sure."

While Ted went to the refrigerator Pauling said to Janey, "Is there something I can do to help out?"

"You can shred some cheese if you want," Janey answered, pointing at the chunk of cheddar on the counter next to a well-used grater. Pauling started the process while Ted handed her a bottle of beer. She raised the bottle, said 'cheers' and took a long drink. Still a little tired from the trip, the beer tasted great. Ice cold.

"Do you normally all eat together?" Pauling asked.

"Hell no," Ted said. "This place is chaotic with everyone on different schedules. We all kind of chip in and grab food or cook whatever's in the fridge. Abner does most of the supply ordering, so we're stuck with whatever's around. It's not like there's a grocery store around the corner."

Just then, Dr. Sirrine emerged from the hallways behind the kitchen. Pauling had a strange notion that he'd been standing there listening and now decided to come into the room. She wasn't sure why she felt that way, but it felt right.

"Yes, I'm in charge of the ordering," he said. "And this is the most important part." He held up a beer from the fridge and also gestured toward some chilled bottles of white wine in the door's shelves and a vast array of red wine on the counter to the left of the fridge.

"Not everyone drinks here," Janey said, rolling her eyes a bit at Dr. Sirrine and Ted. "These guys make it sound like we're a bunch of lushes. But since there isn't a whole lot to do around here after the work is done, let's say that most of us enjoy the cocktail hour on a fairly regular basis."

"Cocktail hours, would be more accurate," Ted said, putting emphasis on the plurality of the word.

He chugged his beer and got another, raised an eyebrow in question at Pauling. She smiled and shook her head. Her beer was still pretty much full.

"So you're here to help with our computer systems?" Janey said.

Pauling heard Ted snicker under his breath.

A quick glance at Janey's wide and expressionless face made Pauling groan inwardly because the picture of innocence was total bullshit. Nathan's efforts to place Pauling here secretly hadn't worked. Pauling instantly knew that no one had bought the cover story.

"That, and more," Pauling said. The rest of them seemed to wait for her to explain, but she didn't. It wasn't a lie. And the tone in her voice conveyed the message that she didn't care what they thought. She was going to do her job and do it right.

Clearly, the message got through because Ted's smirk dropped immediately from his face and Janey quickly became more interested in her meal preparation.

And suddenly, Dr. Sirrine was gone.

CHAPTER SIXTEEN

After dinner, the fajitas were surprisingly tasty, Pauling stopped at the bulletin board in the hallway on the way to her room. There were various schedules posted, some Dilbert cartoons and a few articles on the Bird Conservatory, mostly pertaining to funding issues. There were also a few military articles about various internal notices regarding construction projects on the island.

Pauling went down to her door, unlocked it and stepped into her room. She suddenly had a flashback from college. It felt like a dorm room to her and reminded her of her freshman year at the university. Her roommate had been a strange girl from Oklahoma who spent most of the year at the health clinic on campus. A true hypochondriac. For Pauling during that freshman year, it had been like not having a roommate at all. She remembered initially trying to do everything she could to help the poor girl. It had been a roommate's duty, after all. But by the fifth or sixth mystery illness, Pauling realized the girl was just coping with the transition to college the only way she knew how.

After that recognition became clear, Pauling barely even asked the girl what was going on or how she was feeling.

Now, Pauling locked the door behind her. She glanced at the satellite phone and the computer on her desk and thought about calling Nathan Jones to try to get more information on Jack Reacher. Where was he? He was supposed to get in touch with her once she was on the island, but so far, there had been no word. And she had no way of contacting him.

So instead, Pauling thought about the investigation.

The police report had been a major disappointment. No report, really, at all. No investigation, certainly. It had been deemed a drowning and that was that.

Still, she knew she was going to have to confront the police at some point, if she could dig up some kind of information to get them interested.

But right now, her plan was going to be straightforward. She was going to try to figure out with whom Paige had spent the majority of her time while working here. Once she identified that person, Pauling would go after him or her hard and try to garner as much information as possible. Once she had a better idea of Paige's closest circle, she could rule them all out and go back to Nathan with the most likely answer; that Paige really had drowned.

It was Pauling's opinion that no human being ever really understood another. It was an impossible assumption. Understanding required full knowledge. And no one had full knowledge of another human being. It simply didn't exist. There were things spouses, married for decades, still kept from one another. There was no expiration date on secrets. Pauling suspected that Paige, just like every other human being ever to exist on the planet Earth, had had a few secrets of her own. Nathan was convinced that his daughter was one thing, but the truth was, she was probably that along with a few other things. The world was only black and white in fancy art galleries showcasing the latest avant-garde photographer's work.

In the real world, there were as many different shades of reality as there were people who perceived them. Hell, half the time people had trouble admitting to themselves who they were, how could anyone expect them to be honest with others?

Pauling stretched out on her single bed, amused that her feet nearly hung over the edge and that her mattress felt like a glorified piece of plywood. She stared at the dropped ceiling tile, noticed a brown water stain at the corner of one of the sections.

She pulled Paige's journal off the table next to the bed and opened it to where she'd left off.

The contents continued to be field notes, broken up only occasionally by a sketch of certain plants, or a lizard. Paige had also included observations on the weather, amount of sunlight, and levels of moisture in the soil. There were quite a few notations on specific birds, naturally, most coded in a combination of letters and numbers that were indecipherable to Pauling. She made a mental note to show the codes to Dr. Sirrine and see if he could decipher them for her.

She was just about to close the journal when a section of text centered on the page as opposed to all of the other writing that was flush left caught her eye.

It was four lines, written in the same block letters that Pauling had come to appreciate as the penmanship required of a scientist.

Pauling read the words with great interest.

S *mooth blue oceans of calm*
hidden currents twisting
vestiges of desert guns
here but still there too

She read them two more times and then closed the journal.

One of her literature professors in college had told the class that in his opinion great poetry by itself meant nothing. That there was no internal message required. Rather, the value of a great poem was that it could mean something different to each person who read it. That even if a poem did carry a specific thought, originated by its author, the greatness of the writing was that it had the potential to be interpreted emotionally on a highly individual basis.

A lot of students disagreed, and Pauling knew that some of the other professors argued just the opposite. It was their belief that a good poem conveyed a very specific idea or emotion, one the poet intended to convey with precision.

But the theory of multiple possible interpretations had always stuck with Pauling.

And now, she wondered about the four lines Paige had penned.

It could be about the ocean.

It could be about time.

It could be about the shifting tides of memory and perception.

Or, it could be about a man with blue eyes just back from serving overseas in the military.

CHAPTER SEVENTEEN

It was a horrible night.

She went from being freezing cold to insanely hot. There were bad dreams, along with explosions.

Her eyes snapped open.

She was covered in sweat.

And the explosions weren't just in her dreams. They were outside her window.

She sat up and listened.

Dr. Sirrine had mentioned that the military trained a lot at night. And sure enough, the gunfire was loud and intense. One of the explosions was so close it rattled the walls.

She got out of bed and went to the bathroom, filled a cup with water and drank deeply.

Eventually, she went back to bed and slept for a few hours but when she woke up in the morning, she felt more tired than when she'd gone to sleep.

After an ice-cold shower, Pauling went to the kitchen area and discovered that while there was no organized breakfast, someone had at least made coffee.

It was the large, aluminum tower coffee pot that Pauling

associated with banquet halls and church basement get-togethers. She poured herself a cup and walked over to the living area, to the window that overlooked the cliff's edge and the ocean beyond.

She had to laugh.

This would be primo real estate anywhere else. If, instead of a set of buildings belonging to a wildlife group, it was a six bedroom house in La Jolla, Malibu or Miami with this kind of ocean view it would be worth tens of millions of dollars and owned by a movie star, a professional athlete or a business mogul.

Here, it was just taken for granted.

Outside, behind the main building, Pauling noticed a pair of horseshoe pits and a gas grill. It appeared that was the extent of the entertainment options.

"So I hear you're going out with me today," a voice said behind her. She turned and saw a tiny man, stocky, with a shaved head and chubby cheeks. He had on jeans, hiking boots and a shirt with a vest that had about twenty pockets.

"Gabe Rawlins," he said. He stuck out a thick hand with stubby fingers and Pauling shook it. The hand was warm, almost sweaty, but the grip was like iron.

"Lauren Pauling," she said.

"I see you've got the most important thing for today. Coffee. Lots and lots of coffee."

She smiled. "It's not going to be terribly exciting, is that what you mean?"

Gabe put his hands on his hips and considered her question.

"Let me put it this way. I've had more people fall asleep on me than a hooker at a narcolepsy convention."

He waited for her reaction with obvious expectancy and when she chuckled, he beamed at her.

"You probably had preconceived notions of what bird

people are like," he said. "Which is fine. Because I had a preconceived idea of what a computer geek who was coming to help us out would look like. And boy was I wrong."

Pauling didn't take the bait and easily sidestepped the trap.

"So what exactly is on our schedule today?" she asked. Gabe's face gave away his disappointment at not being able to comment on her appearance, which Pauling knew he was hoping to do.

"Sitting, watching birds and taking notes," Gabe said. "All day. If we really want to get crazy maybe we'll take some soil and plant samples. But I don't want to get your hopes up."

She smiled. "It actually sounds sort of interesting."

"Wow, you're a cheap date," Gabe said.

Again, he looked to her for a reaction and she gave him none.

"Why don't we meet outside in five minutes or so?" he said, glancing at his watch. It was an oversized piece of hardware that must have been able to tell him every scientific measurement there was to make.

He left and walked down the hallway behind the kitchen where Dr. Sirrine had gone. Pauling figured that the men were on one side of the building and the women were on the other. Once again, she couldn't help but compare it to a college dorm.

Pauling went back to her room, grabbed a fleece jacket and a windbreaker. Her plan was to dress in layers while she was here. It seemed like the kind of place where weather could change on a dime.

When she got outside Gabe was already in the truck, an old white Ford with the engine idling. She climbed inside, smelled coffee and cigar or cigarette smoke. Maybe even the hint of marijuana.

Gabe put the truck in gear.

"Just so you know, I tend to say a lot of inappropriate things, but my goal is to never offend," Gabe explained. "So just let me know if I've crossed the line. I'm a bit of a failed comedian if you hadn't already noticed."

"Get out of town," Pauling said.

Gabe grinned at her. "I like you. I think we're going to get along just fine."

CHAPTER EIGHTEEN

A light mist began to cover the windshield and Gabe had to use the wipers to clear it.

"We're going to head to the southwest side of the island, near a place called Horseshoe Canyon. We've got a small bird group there and today's task is to try to determine how well they've been feeding and if there's been any noticeable change in habitat growth."

"Okay."

"We'll start at an observation post but depending on what we see, we may venture into the habitat in order to take some measurements."

They drove on and Pauling was again struck by the landscape. So foreign it almost felt alien. They weren't on a gravel road anymore, this one was plain dirt and she was glad the truck was four-wheel drive. She could imagine some serious storms out here and with the road being little more than mud, a loss of traction could be devastating. Especially as there wasn't a single guardrail on the entire island.

Thankfully, Gabe was a better driver than Dr. Sirrine but sometimes the road went right up to the edge of the cliff and there was nothing between them and the ocean save for a steep cliff of jagged rock. If you lost control and went over the edge there was nothing to stop you from a horrific fall into the ocean.

Twenty minutes later Gabe pulled up to a spot that was marked off from the road. There was a wooden pole stuck into the ground next to something that looked like an overgrown mailbox. A garbage can with a metal lid and a lock and chain was next to it.

Gabe got out and Pauling followed him.

He opened the box and she saw a stack of papers, binders and various implements that looked like they belonged in a hardware store.

Gabe slid one of the binders into his backpack, a sturdy thing made of green burlap.

"Okay, let's go," he said.

He turned and trundled off onto a well-worn foot trail and Pauling walked along behind him. She was glad she had packed a sturdy set of hiking boots. It was cool but not cold. Just a slight chill in the air exacerbated by the slight mist.

Pauling was also glad she'd dressed in layers and only now wished she'd thrown in a baseball cap for good measure.

Well, next time, she thought.

The trail wound down away from the ocean and thick ground cover quickly grew in height.

There were isolated stands of trees, mostly scrub oak and one time Pauling heard something scurry away from them into the underbrush.

Eventually, they made their way to an area roughly six feet by ten feet, cleared, with a trap spread out and an overhang made of tent poles and thick camouflage netting.

It was a lean-to and Gabe slid into one side and Pauling took the other.

Gabe pulled out an enormous set of binoculars and began

to scan the surrounding tree lines. He stopped occasionally to make some notes. He grunted a few times at what he saw.

Pauling sat with her knees up and her arms hugging her legs. She wasn't sure what she was looking at.

"What are you looking for?" she asked.

"Seeing if they're eating," Gabe answered. "That's the big thing. When the bird population almost died out it was because they were starving. The goats and the military had decimated all of the habitat and their prey was almost completely gone. Nowhere to hide, that kind of thing."

Pauling remembered that Dr. Sirrine had told her some of the same details.

"Oh yeah, they're eating well today," Gabe said, looking through the binoculars.

"How can you tell?"

"Take a look."

He handed her the binoculars.

"Okay, look straight out toward that stand of trees."

Once she got herself oriented Pauling was able to bring the group of small oak trees into focus.

"Okay, look at the top of the tree," Gabe said. "And then go down about one branch level."

"Got it," Pauling said.

"Now do you see the lizard impaled on the branch?"

She scanned and was about to say no but then she saw it. She gave a sharp intake of breath. A lizard had literally been skewered onto a vertical, dead branch. A small bird with black and white feathers was picking at its flesh, tearing it away in chunks with its beak.

"You didn't know how the Shrike of San Clemente hunt and eat their prey?" Gabe asked, an amused expression on his face.

"No," Pauling replied truthfully, her voice soft.

"They go after small vertebrates like that native lizard and dive bomb them," Gabe said. His face was alive with a bizarre kind of enthusiasm. "They strike them in the head with their beaks and knock them unconscious. After that, they take them up and impale them on a branch and then slowly pick away at the meat. It sometimes takes days for them to eat one."

"Interesting," Pauling said.

"That's how they got their nickname."

Pauling lowered the binoculars and looked at Gabe.

"What nickname?"

He smiled at her, an odd expression in his eyes. It momentarily gave Pauling a chill.

And then she remembered the name from Paige's journal.

"The Butcher Bird," she said.

"Exactly," Gabe agreed.

CHAPTER NINETEEN

The afternoon saw a slight break in the light rain and the sun even came out briefly before being swallowed once again by a wall of gray in the sky.

Gabe continued to make notes in his field journal, alternating between his binoculars and a camera equipped with an extremely long lens.

"A picture's worth a thousand pages of notes," he said, shaking his hand, tired from writing in his field notebook. Pauling had noted that his handwriting was very similar to Paige's. All caps, block letters, neat and readable. A scientist's penmanship.

Eventually he put away the camera and the binoculars and checked his watch.

"Not a great day to go out and collect anything. Too wet. And with some of the population still actively feeding, not a good idea to disturb them too much."

There was something about the island and its abandoned-planet vibe that was getting to Pauling. It had a sense of lawlessness to it. That observation gave her pause, and she wondered about Paige and the psychological effects, long-term, of being out here. Could it drive someone to murder?

There was a very definite sense of lawlessness here. No highway patrol. No speed traps. No local cops. What, were they going to be pulled over on the way back to the bird headquarters? A suspicious vehicle pulled over by Johnny Law?

Not hardly.

Pauling wondered if that mentality existed for others and to what degree? If there was somebody on the island with bad intentions, a bad guy, how much did they feel they could get away with? Pauling was sure there was a military police presence here, although she imagined it wasn't very large.

In the reports from Nathan, she knew that civilian law enforcement was handled by the Los Angeles County Sheriff's Department, but their nearest office was on Catalina Island, which was some twenty miles away. Which meant there was no civilian police force on San Clemente at all.

She thought back to Nate's reports about the discovery of Paige. It had immediately been deemed a drowning. But how long had it taken the cops to arrive from Catalina Island? A few hours? A day or two? And who watched over the body during that time?

"You look lost in thought," Gabe said.

"Just thinking," she said. "This place seems conducive to thinking. Daydreaming. Wondering."

"It does," Gabe agreed. "I've done fieldwork in a lot of places but nowhere as isolated as this. It's an unusual place."

"It seems almost a little dangerous," she said. "I heard on the plane ride over here that a girl drowned."

Gabe nodded. "Yeah. Her name was Paige. She was a good scientist, very meticulous with her notes and observations."

"How did she drown?"

Gabe shrugged his shoulders. "No one really knows. The

ocean is dangerous around the island, a lot of wicked currents."

"I would never get in that water," Pauling said. "Screw the currents, I'd be worried about the sharks."

Pauling suddenly thought of Paige's poem. It wasn't about Gabe. Gabe had brown eyes.

"We should get back," Gabe said, a bit too abruptly for Pauling's taste. "I think Abner said something about giving you a tour of the place. Fascinating, I'm sure," he said with a forced smile.

They gathered their gear and climbed back into the truck. As they drove, Pauling gazed out at the sea and wondered again what kind of psychological impact there would be if a person had to work here day after day, month after month.

She realized almost immediately how it could make someone feel.

Lonely.

Pauling realized she would feel a lot better if she could find Jack Reacher.

CHAPTER TWENTY

"A h, there you are," Dr. Sirrine said when she and Gabe entered the main building. He was at the table, working on a laptop with a can of Diet Coke next to him.

Dr. Sirrine snapped his laptop closed and got to his feet.

"I want to give you an overview of the rest of the place so you have a better idea of how this whole thing works."

"Sounds good," Pauling said. "Also, is there a place where military police have an office?"

Dr. Sirrine looked strangely at her.

"There are no military police on the island," he said. "But I can take you to the headquarters of the military folks."

"Ok, let's do that after the tour," Pauling said. Certainly the military folks would know where Reacher was.

Dr. Sirrine looked at his watch. "Take five minutes or so to put away your gear and meet me back here," he said.

She went to her room, unlocked it and threw her gear on the bed. Pauling went into the bathroom and splashed some cold water on her face and brushed her teeth.

Pauling went back to the lobby and Dr. Sirrine led her out

of the front door of the building. They followed a stone path around to another long, low aluminum-sided structure.

He opened the door and Pauling was surprised to find the space flooded with a ton of natural light.

She looked up, saw that huge chunks of the ceiling had been cut out and filled with jerry-rigged skylights. They weren't real skylights, but homemade versions built with wood framing and a type of acrylic or hard plastic, mixed in with intersecting sections of camouflage netting. The skylights were clearly not made of glass.

"Hard polypropylene," Dr. Sirrine said, noticing her upward gaze. "Someone tried conventional skylights a few years back and they were destroyed either by a storm or some wayward mortar shells. No idea which story is true."

Pauling wasn't sure if he was kidding or not. After some thought, she realized he wasn't. He wasn't the kind of guy to joke around.

"This is our nursery," he said. He gestured toward multiple rows of unique structures made with a combination of wood, chicken wire and more camouflage netting. Small trees were growing in the space and some of the enclosures were built around segregated shrubbery.

"We've managed to foster several dozen birds and bird families here," he said. "It's been crucial to the repopulation of the island."

They walked through the space and Pauling noted the precision with which the area had been filled out. Everything was neat and clean and well-organized.

"Ted does a great job here, with some assistance from Janey," Dr. Sirrine said. "But Ted's main job is the nursery and he's a natural."

He led through a set of doors at the far end of the building and they passed under an overhang and directly into the next structure.

"This is the herbarium," Dr. Sirrine said. "This is Janey's domain."

Gone was the purely aluminum shed and in its place was a greenhouse of similar size and dimension. When they stepped inside, Pauling immediately felt the cloying moist heat. With the high amount of natural light and the quality of the air, she figured Janey was successful in her efforts.

There were plants along the middle row of tables and various stands, pots and assorted plantings, all fed by a mist of water that rotated in intervals throughout the rows of plants.

"The first step in understanding the decline of the Shrike was to understand the decline of the habitat," Dr. Sirrine said. "The environment was made of native plants, trees and wild grasses. There hadn't really been any introduction of foreign plant life. Once we understood what happened to the native species and what was still happening to them, we would have our first clue as to what was going wrong."

He looked up.

"Oh, there's Janey now," he said.

Janey set down a garden hose and approached them. She had on an old sweatshirt and there was dirt on the side of her face. Her hair was tied back into a short ponytail.

"Hi Abner," she said. "Hey, Pauling."

"How are things going, Janey?" Dr. Sirrine asked.

"Good, we had a bit of a fungus problem on the *Castilleja grisea* seedlings but I think I was able to eliminate most of it."

"Excellent."

"How was your first day in the field?" Janey asked Pauling.

"It was actually very interesting," she said evenly. "I'm enjoying learning more about the kind of work you do out here. And the Shrike is a fascinating bird."

Janey nodded but Pauling could sense the skepticism in

her. Why was this young woman so cynical? Or perceptive, in this case?

"Gabe behaved himself?" Janey asked with a small grin.

"More or less," Pauling answered.

"Some of us are going up to the Salty Crab tonight to grab a drink if you want to come," Janey said.

"Sure. Sounds good." Pauling was anxious to see it. Reacher wasn't exactly a sit-at-the-bar kind of guy, but there weren't any diners on the island, as far as she could tell.

"It's the only bar on the island," Dr. Sirrine added. "The military guys are there all the time so consider yourself warned."

CHAPTER TWENTY-ONE

"There she is," Gabe said. "The world's hottest computer repair person."

They were all standing by the front door, ready to go to the Salty Crab.

"Who was the runner-up?" Pauling asked.

Gabe didn't have a comeback and Ted laughed under his breath.

"Let's go," Janey said in the silence.

"Thanks for waiting," Pauling said.

"No problem," Janey answered and she led the way out the door. They climbed into the same dirty white jeep Dr. Sirrine had picked her up in.

"Is Dr. Sirrine coming?" Pauling asked.

The others chuckled.

"You really have to start calling him Abner," Ted said. "It's throwing me."

"He might join us later," Janey said.

"No, he won't," Gabe answered, shaking his head. "He hardly ever goes there anymore. He doesn't like the clientele."

Gabe's voice became sarcastic at the word.

"The military guys?" Pauling guessed.

"And girls," Ted said. "There are a few women but not many. They can be just as obnoxious as the guys. Abner prefers quiet when he drinks."

Janey visibly stiffened at the way Ted worded the phrase and Pauling wondered if there was more to the story. She would have to figure that out.

It took them less than ten minutes to get to the Salty Crab. From the outside, it looked just like every other structure on the island. A utilitarian, single-story building made with aluminum siding and off-the-rack windows and doors.

There were a half-dozen vehicles in the parking lot, most of them pickup trucks emblazoned with some sort of military emblem or another.

When they exited the jeep, Pauling could hear the music inside.

Gabe paused and turned to Pauling.

"Needless to say, this isn't your average dive bar," he said. "Since this is your first time here all I'll say is to be careful. Some of these guys might be just back from overseas and if they've seen some of the really bad stuff, they aren't necessarily in a great frame of mind."

"And the ones who have been on the island for awhile are generally as aggressive as hell," Janey said.

"She means horny," Gabe countered.

"Got it," Pauling said.

Ted led the way inside.

The door opened into a large room that featured a dozen long wooden tables flanked by heavy wooden chairs. There was a bar with a single bartender manning the operation. A short row of bar stools faced the bar, only one of them occupied.

There was a jukebox in one corner, and a few pinball machines in the other.

Across from the jukebox were two pool tables, one of them being used by two young men in t-shirts and jeans. They stared openly at Pauling.

"They smell fresh blood," Ted said, his voice dry.

A waitress brought a pitcher of beer and four glasses. Ted did the honors and poured everyone a glass.

"To Pauling. May her stay on the island be memorable and productive," Gabe said.

"Cheers," Janey agreed.

They all drank. The beer was cold and tasted fresh. She figured if there was one thing the military guys demanded, it was good booze.

"So what do you think of the Crab?" Janey asked. She peered at Pauling over the rim of her glass.

"It reminds me of a bowling alley," she answered honestly. It really did. The wood floor, scratched and marred. The basic tables. The beer signs, the juke box, the pinball machines.

"Circa twenty years ago," she quickly added.

Gabe laughed. "It really is a place stuck a couple of decades in the past."

"Well, that didn't take long," Janey said.

Pauling heard a voice speak behind her.

"Do we have a new birdie in the nest?"

It was one of the pool players. Up close, Pauling realized he was huge. At least six foot five, two-fifty, with giant shoulders and a narrow waist. He had a tattoo of barbed wire around one of his biceps.

"Clever," Gabe said.

"You want to play some pool?" the big guy said to Pauling. His partner was waiting back at the table.

"No thanks," Pauling said. "Just going to have a drink with my friends. But have you seen Jack Reacher around?"

The big guy looked at her with an odd expression.

"Who?" he asked.

"Never mind," Pauling answered.

The big guy nodded his head and looked at the rest of them like Pauling had just said she was going to dive into a trash dumpster.

"Suit yourself," he said.

He sauntered away.

"Who's Jack Reacher?" Janey asked her.

"Some guy I know who's supposedly working out here on the island."

There was a brief moment of silence and then Ted said, "Get used to it. The attention." Ted lifted his chin toward the military guys.

"At least they didn't use their favorite line," Janey said. "When you turn them down."

"Yeah? What's that?"

Janey smiled.

"Well, here on the island, the men outnumber the women something like fifty to one. So the guys hit on every woman here, pretty much. But when you reject them, they like to remind you that if it weren't for the scarcity of available women, they probably wouldn't be interested in you."

"Wow, that was nicely put," Gabe said.

"That's not what they say," Ted explained. "They have a phrase they love to use."

"Spit it out, guys," Pauling said.

Janey turned to her.

"They like to say, 'You're only a plane ride from ugly.'"

CHAPTER TWENTY-TWO

Pauling swung out of bed, made her way to the shower and let the hot water beat down on her. She toweled off, dressed in jeans, a sweatshirt and hiking boots and went into the kitchen area.

The giant coffee pot had already worked its magic and Pauling poured herself a cup. She carried it outside and walked along the edge of the property's border, stopping occasionally to look out at the ocean. It was a cool morning with a gauzy layer of clouds hovering above the sapphire blue water. A bird flew overhead, followed by the sound of an automatic weapon firing off rounds.

Morning on San Clemente Island.

So far, not a single person had heard of Jack Reacher. Pauling wondered about Nathan Jones and his motivation for bringing her out here.

Ultimately, it didn't matter. Pauling was hooked. She wanted to find out what had happened to Paige Jones on this weird, mysterious island.

One way or another, she would get answers.

With or without Reacher.

Eventually, she finished her coffee and headed back to the Nest.

She walked inside and saw Dr. Sirrine – Abner – sitting at the table with a short, squat fireplug of a man with a head of steel cut hair and a face that looked like a slab of cement.

The man had on a dark blue t-shirt with a gold crest over the breast pocket and a pair of khaki pants with multiple pockets. He had on camouflage hunting boots.

"Pauling," Abner said. "Someone here would like to meet you."

She put her cup of coffee on the counter and walked over to them. Both men stood and the short one stuck out his hand.

"Ma'am, I'm Commander Wilkins," he said. His voice perfectly fit his gravelly appearance. "But you can call me Bill."

"Hi Bill, I'm Lauren Pauling."

The man smiled, but he did it more with his eyes than his mouth. His face was leathery with deep creases. He had blue eyes and Pauling could see the lively sense of humor behind them.

"The boys up at the Crab didn't know your name," Wilkins said. "But you sure fit the description."

Ordinarily, a statement like that would be followed by a leer. But somehow, Wilkins pulled it off and Pauling didn't sense any creepiness.

Now it was her turn to smile.

"So are you Commander of San Clemente or something else?" she asked.

"Yes," Abner stepped in. He sounded nervous, as if Pauling might say something to upset Wilkins.

"Bill is in charge of everything, and everyone, on the island. Technically." Abner added that qualifier at the end, probably referencing the bird personnel. Wilkins wasn't in charge of them. Of course, being in charge of someone and having power over them are two different things.

"Great," Pauling said. "Do you have any idea where I can find Jack Reacher?" she asked.

"Jack Reacher? I don't know anyone by that name," he answered.

And Pauling felt like she finally had her answer.

They all sat down at the table.

"I like to come out and catch up with Abner whenever he's got someone new on his team," Wilkins explained. "Communication is the key to everything we do. So if something ever comes up, I know we're all on the same playing field and I know who the players are."

"Do things come up often?" Pauling asked, making sure her voice sounded as innocent as possible.

"What do you mean?" Abner interjected.

Wilkins just smiled at her. He knew exactly what she meant.

"Well," Pauling said, "It sounded like you were saying that if there's a problem between the bird people and the military, you like to know who everyone is ahead of time."

It was a guess, but Pauling figured that's why the commander was here.

She had no doubt that the men from the bar last night had talked about her. And at his age, she figured Wilkins wasn't here to ask her out on a date.

"No, not much comes up out here," Wilkins said. "No real problems between the two groups of people. Unless you count my two divorces," he said, followed by a wink.

"You're serious, aren't you?" she asked, knowing he was.

"Afraid so," Wilkins answered. "I could never keep my hands off of those pretty birdies. Should've known better," he shook his grizzled head.

Pauling wasn't taken in by his *aw shucks* attitude. He

looked like the kind of guy who wasn't really an administrator. In his day, he'd probably conquered some territories all by himself. A Special Ops guys for sure.

"It really is an interesting dynamic," Pauling ventured. "Some of the deadliest military personnel in the world cuddled up with a group of scientists. I'm sure it could make for some unique issues."

"Over the years all of the bugs have been worked out," Abner said. "Everything has always run very smoothly, at least since I've been here."

Wilkins nodded. "Abner keeps his folks in line, and I do the same with mine. We're all professionals."

Wilkins got to his feet.

"Well, I've got to get going," he said. "Pauling, if you ever want to come up to my HQ I'd love to give you the cook's tour of the island and show you what we do here. That is, if Abner ever stops working you like a dog. He's a real slave driver, I hear."

Abner chuckled and shook his head.

"I would like that, Bill," Pauling said.

And she meant it.

CHAPTER TWENTY-THREE

"Has there?"

Dr. Sirrine had just started to get up but Pauling stopped him with the tone of her voice. She was at the coffee pot and she raised her head at him to see if he wanted some. He held up his hand to say no. She filled her own and sat down across from him.

"Has there what?" he answered, without conviction. Pauling could see his reticence a mile away.

"Has there ever been any problems between the naturalists and the military people?" she said, spelling it out for both of their benefit.

Dr. Sirrine let out a long sigh.

"Yes and no," he finally said.

"What does that mean?"

He sat back and folded his hands across his stomach, and seemed to look past Pauling out toward the island beyond.

"As far as the military folks see it, this is their island," he explained. "They only humor us because they have to and they don't want the bad press back home to talk about them destroying an endangered species."

"That makes sense."

"But make no mistake," he continued. "They feel the work they do is the only work that matters here. They think what we do, running around taking care of these little birds and the little trees and shrubs they depend on is a big joke."

Pauling nodded. She'd worked with a lot of military guys and knew that what Dr. Sirrine was saying was true.

"As far as the military thinks, the work they do keeps the country safe," he continued. "They're providing us with the freedom we need to live our lives. It's the most important job in the world and they believe we take it all for granted."

There was some truth in that belief, Pauling thought.

"And because of that," Dr. Sirrine said. "We ought to get down on our knees and thank the Lord every day for the guys with guns who take care of us."

"So they think they're better than us?" Pauling asked.

"Yes."

"Above the law?" Pauling probed. She knew the answer, but wanted to hear what Dr. Sirrine thought. After all, he had worked closely with Paige and any insight into his view of the world would help her investigation. If nothing else, it would help point her in the right direction.

Dr. Sirrine shrugged his shoulders.

Pauling was surprised that there wasn't any anger in his voice, considering the net of what he was saying.

"On the one hand, as an American, I believe what they do is essential to our survival as a country. Our peace, our prosperity, our very way of life. Absolutely," Dr. Sirrine said. "On the other hand, losing a species, any species, for eternity, is a pretty big deal, too."

"In other words," Pauling said, "It doesn't have to be one is more important than the other. They both can co-exist."

"Yes, that's how I see it," he said. "But they don't."

Pauling considered what he was saying.

"So I asked you if there had ever been any problems between us and them. You said yes and no. What did you mean by that?"

"My point is that if there is a problem, whoever from our side that's involved is usually promptly escorted off the island," Dr. Sirrine said. "End of problem."

"I see."

"Luckily, I've been here for a number of years and the biggest problems tend to be when people drink too much and they get into arguments. Even then it usually doesn't get physical because we're obviously overmatched."

Pauling thought of the huge guy from last night. He could have pulverized Ted, Gabe and Dr. Sirrine with one hand tied behind his back.

"What about problems between men and women?" Pauling asked. "Whenever you have a shortage of women and some hot-blooded young men who may or may not be returning or going to a battlefield, you could have some pretty big problems."

"Like I said, it hasn't happened yet," Dr. Sirrine said. "Or at least recently. Because everyone is very careful, especially on my team. I've made it a priority for everyone who works for me to understand that with absolute clarity. And you should be, too."

"Was Paige careful?" she asked.

It looked like Dr. Sirrine had been punched in the solar plexus.

"What kind of question is that?" he asked. His face was pale and she could see the anger in his eyes.

"I'm asking you if Paige ever had any problems with people in the military here on the island."

He looked at her a long time and finally let out a deep breath.

"No," he said. "Not to my knowledge." Which, for some

reason, struck Pauling as something someone would say in a court of law. As if they were on trial. And it was a phrase a lot of people used when they weren't really telling the whole truth.

Dr. Sirrine got up and walked to his hallway, shutting the door behind him.

From what she understood, Dr. Abner Sirrine was one of the world's leading experts on Loggerhead Shrikes and, in particular, the San Clemente Shrike.

Which was a good thing.

Pauling got up and dumped the rest of her coffee into the sink.

Because he was one of the worst liars she'd ever seen.

CHAPTER TWENTY-FOUR

P auling went back to her room, changed out of her jeans and hiking boots into a pair of sweatpants and trail-running shoes. She grabbed a map of the island and found Janey in the herbarium.

"Is this a good place to run?" she asked, using her finger to trace a route on the map. She had done some research on the plane and knew that the trail ran along the beach where Paige's body had been found. Any evidence was long gone, of course, but she wanted to see the place with her own eyes.

She watched as Janey appraised the route.

"Yeah, that's fine," she said and tapped a finger, one with dirt packed beneath the fingernail, toward a horizontal line on the trail.

"Just do NOT cross that line," she said. A speck of dirt remained on the map where Janey's finger had been.

"That's where they do their private training, the endurance testing and some live fire trial exercises," Janey explained. "Some of the guys they occasionally get in are young. Most are seasoned but it always seems like someone's either a bad shot or there's the occasional ricochet."

Janey's eyes seemed to linger on the area of the trail where Paige had been found.

"I'll look at it as an adrenaline boost," Pauling said. "Who knows, maybe I'll run faster."

Janey looked like she was going to say something but stopped. She turned away, then changed her mind and turned back.

"Be careful," she said.

Pauling said she would, folded the map up and put it in the pocket of her sweatpants and set out on a run once she got back out on the main road.

The road was called Perimeter Drive and naturally it ran along the contour of the island. The entrance to the footpath was less than a mile from the Nest.

It was strange to be working out without music but Pauling wanted to be able to hear anything that was going on. Especially if she heard rifle fire that sounded like it might be a hair too close.

Once she was warmed up she set out at a slow jog, enjoying the feel of the moisture in the air, the soft sea breeze that always seemed to be blowing.

She found the turnoff and went down the path, a trail of hard-packed dirt and small stones.

It skirted the edge of the cliff and she had to remind herself that if she went over the side, no one would find her for a long time.

She lengthened her stride, glad to be running again. When she'd worked at the Bureau she'd run every day and had come to crave the exercise, her antidote for stress.

Pauling ran easily, eating up the miles, lost in the stark beauty of the scenery. She had once run on the beach in Malibu and not only was this breathtaking in its unique way, she had this all to herself.

There was nothing marking the area where Paige's body

had been found but Pauling recognized it right away from the photographs in the documents Nathan had given her. She slowed to a walk and went to the water's edge.

The air seemed to turn colder all around her and this close to the water she felt its immense power. The waves crashed into the surf with thunderous regularity she could feel in her knees. Pauling put her hand down and the water was ice cold.

No way Paige would swim in this stuff.

It was not the calmer water of a hotel swimming pool, either. It was a churning type of sea with thick waves, sea lions and kelp out in the distance. It didn't even seem right to call it a beach. This was the real deal. The Pacific Ocean in all its unspoiled beauty and ferocity.

Nathan was right.

Paige would never have gone willingly into this water.

"Watch yourself," a voice said behind her.

Startled, Pauling turned.

A man, also in running gear and slightly out of breath with a fine sheen of sweat on his forehead stopped a few feet from her.

He was strikingly handsome and his perfect teeth gleamed in the gray air.

"There's a hell of an undertow just a few feet out," he said. "If it grabs ahold of you, you don't have a chance."

He stepped closer and a slight chill ran through Pauling's body.

He had the most beautiful pair of blue eyes she had ever seen.

CHAPTER TWENTY-FIVE

"I'm Michael Tallon," he said. He stuck out a hand and Pauling shook it. It was warm and strong but not wet. She had a feeling her hand was sweaty. On his other wrist was an impressive watch, with a thick face and steel bracelet.

"Pauling," she said. "Thanks for the warning."

"It's deceptive," Tallon responded. "The undertow. Guys are always surprised when we get them in the water and it starts pulling at them."

"What do they do?"

"We teach them to swim diagonally, as opposed to directly against the undertow. You have a better chance of swimming out of the current that way. We've had some strong swimmers take it on. And they lost every time."

For a moment, they both stood and looked out at the water.

"It's a Ball," he said.

Pauling looked at him.

He lifted his wrist. "My watch. You were looking at it. A

Ball Engineer Hydrocarbon NEDU. NEDU stands for Navy Experimental Dive Unit."

"So you're Navy?" she asked.

"Sort of," he responded.

"And there was the girl who drowned here, right? This is where they found her body?"

Tallon stiffened at the question, and for a moment the nice guy was gone. His expression had hardened and his mouth had formed a thin line.

"Yeah," he said. "And they didn't find her. I did."

"You found her?" Pauling asked, wondering if the name Michael Tallon had rang any bells with her. Had it been in the police report?

"I run here practically every morning," he explained. "It was not good."

Pauling was about to ask him if he had known Paige, but he cut her off with a quick question of his own.

"So you're with the bird folks?" he asked. There was a small smile on his face.

"You look like you already know the answer to that. What, the guys at the Salty Crab?"

He nodded, a bit sheepish.

She shook her head. "Don't you guys have anything else to do than talk about every new woman who shows up at the bar? What, have you got a web cam there?"

He laughed, and Pauling was struck again by his good looks.

"Hey, I know we just met, but are you hungry? I was going to the cafeteria to get some lunch."

A bit abrupt, but Pauling had to admit, she was hungry. And, more than a little intrigued.

"Sure."

They agreed that Tallon would pick her up at the Nest, so Pauling went back and changed out of her running gear and jumped in the shower. Afterward, she toweled off, threw on a pair of jeans and a fleece pullover and went back outside to find Michael Tallon waiting for her in a military jeep.

She climbed inside, just as Dr. Sirrine appeared in the doorway. He looked at her with an odd expression on his face. Pauling waved, and Dr. Sirrine waved back as Tallon pulled away from the Nest onto Perimeter Drive.

"Have you eaten at the cafeteria yet?" Tallon asked.

"No."

"Well, the good news is, it's the best food on the island," he said.

"And the bad news is that it's the only food on the island?" she guessed.

He laughed. "Yeah, you've heard that one, huh? Well, technically, the other food on the island is the bar menu at the Crab. Which is actually better than the cafeteria, but the Crab's not open yet."

"The Crab's not open?" Pauling asked. "That puts a pretty big hole in the entertainment options for the guys, doesn't it?"

"It does," Tallon admitted. "If there is a silver lining though, it's that the cafeteria actually has a salad bar that's at least serviceable. Everything else there, well, I would tread with caution."

They followed the road down to a slight valley and Pauling saw a cluster of military buildings, one of them actually made with brick as opposed to the island's ubiquitous aluminum siding. The brick building also had real windows that looked out across the road to the ocean.

Tallon pulled the jeep into a parking space in front of the brick building and shut off the car.

"This is it," he said.

Pauling followed him inside and saw the long bank of counters serving an open space filled with tables and chairs.

Across from them was a bank of food stations, complete with sneeze guards and another station that looked like it dispensed soft drinks.

It smelled like a mixture of meat and cabbage.

"Just for fun, go take a look at the food at the buffet," Tallon said.

She swung by and saw only three of the ten or so metal trays had food in them. And each one was a mysterious meat swimming in a slightly different colored gravy.

Pauling quickly joined Tallon at the salad bar. He had a plate and tray ready for her.

"I'm a big fan of mysteries," she said, accepting the tray from him. "But in book form. Not when it comes to food."

"I'm surprised you didn't run out the door," he said.

He laughed and she was struck again by those blue eyes. She wondered again if they were the eyes Paige had written about in her journal. Pauling cautioned herself not to push it. Let things happen naturally and the answers would come.

The salad bar would have been considered average back on the mainland, but out here it looked fantastic to Pauling. She took a mixture of lettuce, some chickpeas, shredded parmesan, olives and sunflower seeds. Finally, she added a light drizzle of olive oil and balsamic vinegar.

Tallon picked out a smaller table next to a window. The view was dynamite, Pauling noticed. She would never get tired of the expanse of ocean just above the horizon.

"So tell me about finding Paige," Pauling said. If he was surprised that she knew Paige's name, he covered it well.

Tallon shook his head. "Pretty bad. I mean, I've seen a lot of things, considering what I do. But, it wasn't good."

"Is that because you knew her?" she asked. It was meant to throw him off guard and it worked. Even though it was a guess, Pauling's instincts told her she was right.

Tallon looked at her, his face difficult to read.

"No," he finally said. "I didn't recognize her. It's just there's a difference between seeing a soldier who's been killed. They chose to be in the fight, whether they're the good guy or the bad guy. But a civilian is always very difficult. A very different experience."

She listened as he explained how he contacted the commander of the island, and showed the investigating authorities where the body was.

Pauling noticed that he hadn't confirmed or denied that he had known Paige. She decided to let it go, for the moment.

"So was it a shark attack?" she asked.

"Sure looked like it," he said. Which wasn't really answering the question.

"Did you think she was swimming?" Pauling asked, and then pointed out at the ocean. "Out there? Water's awfully cold. The dangerous undertow. Sharks."

He shrugged his shoulders. "I don't know."

Pauling munched on some of her salad and then put down her fork and took a drink of water.

"So how did you know Paige?" she finally asked.

"I didn't really," he said. "Just saw her a few times at the Crab, maybe bought her a drink. I don't remember."

If he was lying, Pauling couldn't tell. Plus, she had no way of knowing for sure that Paige's journal was referencing Michael Tallon. It stood to reason there was more than one man on the island with blue eyes and maybe even then it wasn't someone on San Clemente. What if Paige had been remembering someone from her past? From before San Clemente Island?

"I already know the answer, but do you know if Jack Reacher is around?"

Tallon's face took on a puzzled expression.

"Reacher? Why would he be here?"

"You know him?" Pauling was surprised. She'd expected another negative reply.

"Not really, but I know of him. He's Army, though. An MP, right?"

"He was," she said. "He's out now."

"Then he definitely wouldn't be here. But I can tell you that if he was here, I would definitely know it."

He squinted at her.

"Why are you looking for Reacher?"

She looked out the window.

"I'm not," she said.

CHAPTER TWENTY-SIX

Something was different.

Pauling noticed it the minute she stepped through the door. It wasn't that it looked different to her, it was a scent she didn't recognize.

It was the smell that tipped her off and it was an odd observation considering she'd only been here a couple of days and was still getting used to her surroundings.

But it wasn't the kind of vague change that could have resulted from someone mopping the hallway floor and the smell coming into the room under the door.

It was more a sense of something having been disturbed and their presence lingering.

What had they been looking for?

The journal.

Paige's journal. Pauling crossed the room and grabbed it from the night table, anxious to see if there was anything about it that would tell her if it had been read. It didn't look any different. Nor did it feel unusual and she saw no signs that pages had been removed. Of course, there was no way for her to determine if it'd been read or photographed or scanned for that matter.

She hadn't really been here that long, but the act of someone breaking into her room felt like an invasion of privacy. Pauling had the shitty sense of being victimized. Even though the room felt as if it belonged to somebody else, the whole thing unsettled her.

Considering that when Nathan first hired her for this case she had thought the idea of foul play was all in his imagination. Pauling had genuinely believed that her investigation would produce confirmation of an accident.

Nothing more.

But seeing the water and feeling how cold it actually was on her bare skin, seeing the energy of the waves, how wild and how desolate it was had all shocked her.

The idea of Paige going out for a swim seemed ludicrous to her.

And now this. Someone, she was nearly positive, had gone through her belongings, searching for something.

How curious could someone be to actually break into the room of a new employee of the Bird Conservatory?

Sure, there were extremely nosy people everywhere on this earth. However the unwelcome invasion also made sense if the person looking through her stuff was the same one who had something to do with Paige's death.

The image of Dr. Sirrine standing at the door watching her drive off with Michael Tallon suddenly flashed across Pauling's mind. It would have been the perfect opportunity for him, or someone else, to run back to her room and find a way in. Maybe they had an extra key.

For the first time Pauling wished she had been able to bring her gun. But the rules had been clear: no firearms brought onto San Clemente Island.

How ironic on an island surrounded by armed men she

was defenseless other than her intellect and an ability to fight. She closed and locked the door, changed into a t-shirt and sweatpants and laid on the bed. She thought about lunch with Michael Tallon. It'd been pleasant and almost refreshing to talk with somebody other than the people from the Nest.

Or was it just that he was a very good-looking man and she was lonely?

Pauling would have to be very careful from here on out. And she decided that the break-in made it the perfect time for her to take the investigation to the next level.

CHAPTER TWENTY-SEVEN

I n her previous life Pauling was all about the dossier. Hunting, compiling information, targeting, creating psychological makeups; it was all about what she had done for a living.

And she was good at it.

Nathan, being Nathan, had supplied her with an extensive collection of background information. She had pored over those files but they provided mostly surface information. Pauling needed more. She needed the kind of information that wasn't available on public databases.

Pauling opened up her laptop and connected to the Wi-Fi, then joined the network called BirdsnestOne.

Even though the laptop was encrypted, Pauling was fairly certain that somewhere someone was watching what she was about to type. She only hoped that they weren't watching too carefully.

So she wrote a chatty email to Blake completely unlike her regular tone of voice and told a rambling story about how much fun she was having and listed off the people she met in a witty way.

But, in the process, she was sure to include both the first and last name.

For instance, she talked about the interesting Dr. Abner Sirrine. She told him about a funny story going to the Salty Crab with Gabe Rawlins, Janey Morris and Ted Fargo. Her lunch with Michael Tallon was included along with a description of meeting Bill Wilkins, Commander of San Clemente.

And then at the end of her note to Blake she talked about the one drawback to the island was a sense of sensory deprivation and a lack of information.

Blake already knew what she was doing here. He knew what her mission was. But she wanted to leave no room for misunderstanding. She needed to find more about the people she'd met and Blake was a shortcut.

She fired off the email and then closed her browser. She spent the next hour creating specific files for each person on the list. Pauling wrote down everything she knew about each person, described her interactions with each person thus far, and then left room for information from Blake. She intended to continue to investigate and each new piece of information would be added to the appropriate dossier.

It was how she liked to work and would make things easier when she was trying to formulate theories on what may or may not have happened.

Finally, she closed her laptop.

It would take some time for Blake to read her email and do his investigations.

In the meantime, she would continue to dig. And, in the process, hopefully find out who had broken into her room.

CHAPTER TWENTY-EIGHT

P auling walked into the kitchen, opened the fridge and saw a bottle of white wine with a cork in it. She filled a glass three quarters full and walked to the picture window in the living area.

Outside, she saw Janey sitting on the picnic bench looking out at the ocean. Pauling saw an opportunity because if Paige had talked to anyone out here it would've been a woman. And if Paige had been friends with Janey, Janey would be the perfect resource to get more information.

Pauling opened the door, stepped outside and felt the cool ocean breeze, tasted the salt in the air. It had rained earlier in the day and now the grass was wet and the sky had a tinge of orange from the early day shower.

"Mind if I join you?" Pauling asked.

Janey turned and looked at her. She had an odd expression on her face as if she'd been thinking about something that had deeply upset her.

"No, no problem," Janey said.

Pauling took her glass and sat on the picnic table next to

Janey. She didn't say anything, just joined her and looked out toward the water.

"I just saw a great white shark make a snack out of a sea lion," Janey said, her tone very matter-of-fact.

"Does that happen very often?" Pauling asked. "Early evening they start feeding, right?"

"Oh, it happens all the time but you're lucky to see it. Then again, you see a lot of things out here," Janey said.

Pauling wondered what she meant by that. She noticed Janey had a glass of wine in her hand, too.

"Did you know Paige Jones very well?" Pauling asked.

Janey laughed.

"You aren't really here to look at our computer systems, are you?" Janey said.

"Well, I am collecting data if that's what you're asking," Pauling said.

Janey laughed again. "Okay," she said.

Pauling saw a dark shadow pass about 600 feet from the shore. It cruised slowly and at first she thought it was a school of fish and then her breath caught in her throat.

"Is that the shark?"

"It sure is."

Pauling watched as the shadow slowly disappeared.

"I didn't know Paige very well, actually," Janey said, finally answering the question. "We talked occasionally being the only women here at the Nest. But we were both very private people and the conversations never really got too personal."

"Did you see anything out of the ordinary? Anything that made you think somebody would have wanted to hurt Paige?"

Janey shook her head. "No. I didn't see anything out of the ordinary," she said. "But honestly, everything out here is abnormal. This is an unusual place. I mean, think about it. A group of people obsessed with a tiny bird. Academics, really, who spent most of their lives with their noses in thick textbooks studying arcane patterns of wildlife." As she talked, she gestured with the wineglass in her hand. "And now, out here, they're surrounded by men who, for the most part, have a very basic education but extensive knowledge of how to kill people, shoot guns, blow things up and make their enemies disappear."

Janey finished her outburst and looked at Pauling. She was smiling, but there was a strange energy behind it, powered by emotion.

Pauling hid her curiosity by taking a sip of wine.

"So I guess the question is, since you're out here and asking questions about Paige, do you think it wasn't really a drowning?"

"No, I'm not saying that, nor do I have any evidence of that," Pauling answered. "I'm just curious about what happened. What was she really doing out there? This doesn't seem like the kind of place a young woman who doesn't like the water would decide to go out and swim."

"Some of us thought the same thing," Janey said. "We tried to tell them but nobody seemed too interested in our information."

Pauling already knew there wasn't anything in the police report interviews with Paige's co-workers.

"Was there anything you can think of?" Pauling asked, sensing there was a lot more Janey had to say. She just didn't seem to be ready to divulge.

"Look, I can tell you this," Janey said. "It did seem like there were an awful lot of nights where Paige didn't come home. Back to the Nest. Now no one here is a babysitter or a warden. And in fact, there is a rich history of young women coming here to study birds ending up getting a very close-up study of the anatomy of some of these young military guys."

"I see," Pauling said.

"There isn't a lot to do on this fucking island," Janey said.

"I couldn't blame her. If that many guys were to hit on me, I probably would spend a lot fewer nights here too."

She got to her feet and tossed the rest of her wine onto the grass. Pauling wondered if she didn't want to drink anymore, or if the conversation had caused her to lose her desire.

"Okay, I've got to go tend to my plants. Good luck collecting your data," she said. She smiled at Pauling and it was a friendly smile, but with an edge.

Pauling was glad they had connected. Janey left and she looked out at the ocean, at the broad expanse of silver water stretching toward the distant horizon.

Instead of the beauty of the image, Pauling found herself looking in the water for shadows.

CHAPTER TWENTY-NINE

The wine tasted really good so Pauling afforded herself another glass. She sat outside and watched the sun slowly sink below the horizon. The sunsets were spectacular here. When the case wrapped up, if it ever did to anyone's satisfaction, she was going to miss the sunsets. Pauling highly doubted she'd see any again so stunning.

Pauling went back inside to the corkboard that held the keys to the conservatory's vehicles and selected the white jeep that Dr. Sirrine had picked her up in when she'd first come to the island.

She went outside, fired it up and there was a rap on the window that startled her. She jumped.

"Hey, are you going up to the Salty Crab?" Gabe Rawlins looked in at her, a big grin on his cherubic face.

"Yeah, hop in," Pauling said.

Gabe opened the door and slid into the passenger seat. Pauling pulled out of the driveway of the Nest and minutes later they arrived at the Salty Crab, parked and went inside.

There were a few guys sitting at various tables, another group of men shooting pool.

Gabe and Pauling went to the bar, each ordered a beer and sat down near one of the picture windows.

"So what do you think of this whole thing so far?" Gabe said.

"What do you mean?" Pauling answered.

Gabe shrugged his shoulders. "Oh, I don't know," he said. "I guess I'm just wondering since you're new to this and you just met everybody what do you think? Anything strike you as odd? What do you think of all these people? Dr. Sirrine? Ted? Janey?"

Pauling smiled. "Everybody seems cool," she said. "I guess the big question is what do you think of everybody? You've been here longer than I have."

Gabe took a long drink of his beer, which was already almost empty. He had pounded that beer fast. "To be honest I think you got a bunch of second-rate scientists stationed to this outpost because they're losers." He nearly spat the words at Pauling.

"I appreciate you being direct."

"More like being honest," he said. He stood with his empty bottle and Pauling tossed down the rest of her beer. She'd better slow down or she'd get trashed. Best not to try to match Gabe beer for beer.

Gabe went and brought two more beers back to the table.

When he sat down, Pauling asked him, "So how well did you know Paige?"

He shrugged his shoulders as if it was a subject he was tired of discussing. "I hit on her a couple of times," he said. "She wasn't interested, if you can believe that," he said, his voice rich with sarcasm.

He nodded his head toward the military guys sitting over at the tables and playing pool. "She seemed more interested in those kind of guys. You know, ripped bodies, raging hard-ons and IQs in the 70s."

Pauling reconciled the answer with what Janey had told her. Gabe put his beer down on the table and toyed with the napkin underneath it.

Gabe looked up at the man who had suddenly appeared at their table. He was a young guy in a t-shirt and jeans with tattoos covering both arms. He was carrying a tray with three Dixie cups on it.

"Just thought you two might like something stronger than your beers," he said, but his eyes were locked on Pauling. He ignored Gabe completely.

"How thoughtful," Gabe said.

"My name's Tom," he said, and stuck his hand out toward Pauling. She shook it and then picked up one of the Dixie cups.

Pauling hadn't done a shot of liquor in years but she raised the Dixie cup toward Tom and Gabe and tossed it down.

Tequila.

Not her favorite.

Pauling was starting to feel lightheaded.

Tom was looking at her and she realized she hadn't said her name.

"I'm Pauling," she said.

"We were kind of in the middle of something, Tom," Gabe said.

Tom ignored Gabe.

"Thanks for the shot," Pauling said. "But we were talking about some private stuff."

Tom smirked at both of them and then joined his buddies at their table, all of them turning and looking openly at Pauling.

She looked down and saw a slip of paper with a cell phone number on it next to the tray.

Pauling waited until Gabe took a drink of his beer and his eyes were tilted to the ceiling to slide the slip of paper into her hand.

"Want to get out of here?" she asked.

"Sure."

They went up to the bar and got four beers to go which Pauling didn't know was a possibility. They walked out to the jeep and Pauling gave the keys to Gabe.

"You better drive," she said.

They got inside and Gabe immediately cracked a beer.

"Can I show you something totally bizarre?" he asked.

"Sure," she said. "Why the hell not?"

CHAPTER THIRTY

"They call it Rag City," Gabe said.

They had wound their way around the island in the dark, the only light provided was from the headlights, but with the nature of the twisting road, it was easy to become disoriented.

Of course, the alcohol and pot didn't help, either, Pauling mused. She was starting to feel a little carsick. Or just plain sick.

Pauling had no idea where they were or where they were going. It seemed as if Gabe had come to this place quite a few times because he knew exactly how to get there despite the lack of road signs.

"I thought we weren't supposed to wander off from the main roads," Pauling said. "Aren't there guys with guns training at night all over the place shooting their guns and blowing shit up?"

Gabe chugged the rest of his beer. He turned to her.

"Sure, that's what makes this little outing so interesting," he said. "I've always found the idea that I could be shot at any moment kind of invigorating. It gets the juices flowing."

Gabe slammed on the brakes and they skidded to a stop. A cloud of dust overtook them. Gabe left the headlights on and the twin beams of light shot through the dust cloud and illuminated some vague shapes in the distance.

Pauling got out of the jeep and in the dim light saw something that shocked her.

It was a town.

An actual little city block.

Although it was dark she could certainly make out the rows of buildings, the narrow streets running between them, and the size of the place to make her feel like it was a real community.

Sans any people.

"What the hell?" she said.

Gabe laughed. "Come on, I'll show you," he said.

He grabbed himself a new beer and offered one to Pauling but she didn't take it. She'd had enough. She was already walking a little unsteadily on her feet.

Gabe confidently walked ahead and was even whistling a tune. It sounded like a Cat Stevens song.

They walked around the edge of the first building and found themselves in the middle of the street. Pauling's eyes were adjusting to the darkness and combined with a sliver of moonlight, she could see pretty well.

"They use this for training," Gabe explained. "This is supposed to look like a little neighborhood in Iraq or Afghanistan. Except without all of the bad guys."

They strolled up the street and there was enough light so Pauling could see a few feet inside the buildings. They were empty except for structural elements like support beams and staircases.

"How big is this place?" Pauling asked.

"It's really just a couple of city blocks. But they keep adding on to it all the time," Gabe said. "You can hear the engineers up here working on it constantly. The rumor is they had some FBI guys out here last week."

Pauling almost wondered out loud if she would recognize any of them.

"Yeah," Gabe said. "Try to watch where you step. Supposedly there's unexploded ordnance all over the place."

"Great," Pauling said.

"Hey, I want to show you something," he said.

He turned down one alley and then another and went into a building. He used the flashlight app on his phone and waved it around the middle of the room. There was a couch and a couple of chairs. Pauling's foot scraped the floor and a bunch of brass scattered around the space.

Empty shell casings, she realized.

Gabe sat down on the couch and she could see him drinking a beer thanks to just a touch of moonlight filtering in through one of the windows. Although there wasn't an actual glass window but rather a square opening in the wall of concrete.

Pauling went and stood by the couch and suddenly felt Gabe's hand on her ass. She took a step away.

"Hey," she said.

"What? You got a great ass," he said. He laughed a little and drank again from his bottle of beer. "Here we are, alone in the big city, it's so romantic."

"Thanks, but–"

"But what?" Gabe stood and walked toward her and she held her ground. He went to put his arms around her and she put her hand directly on his chest and pushed him back.

"Gabe, I don't know what you had in mind by bringing me up here but whatever you're planning, it isn't going to happen," she said.

There was silence from him and then he turned and hurled his beer bottle against the concrete wall where it shattered. Little bits of glass rained down on the concrete floor and their echoes filled the air.

"Christ, I hate this fucking place," he said.

And then he was gone. Pauling waited a moment and then walked out of the building and into the alley. She saw no one. She tried to make her way back to the jeep but took a wrong turn and ended up walking the long way around the building. She heard an engine rev and tires spinning out.

When she got to where the jeep had been parked it was gone.

She stood there, waiting.

What could she do?

Suddenly a jolt of electricity went down her back. When Gabe had flashed his cell phone camera in the room there'd been a brief glimpse of some graffiti on the wall, and in the darkness the image popped back into Pauling's mind.

It hadn't sunk in because a moment later she was fighting off Gabe.

Now, she raced back to the building recognizing it in the dark as best she could. She went into the room and used her phone's flashlight on the wall.

It wasn't there.

She thought for a moment and realized she might not be in the right spot. She had to go back and figure out exactly where Gabe had been standing.

Pauling retraced her steps and did it again. This time the light illuminated some writing on the wall. She walked toward it with her flashlight app slowly gaining in intensity until she stood before it.

She examined the wall and her breath caught in her throat.

PJ was here.

Paige Jones.

CHAPTER THIRTY-ONE

G abe came back.

Pauling wasn't surprised, she had pretty good instincts when it came to people and he seemed like the type who would come to his senses. Plus, he was a little drunk and a little high, but Pauling didn't think he was cruel.

He pulled up and she opened the door.

"Sorry about that," he mumbled as she climbed in. "I just got a little crazy. You know, sometimes those guys at the Crab just piss me off and I wonder why I'm not more aggressive. And then something like this happens and I know why."

"You just had on your beer goggles," she said. Gabe chuckled and they pulled out of Rag City with a spray of dirt and gravel.

"Seriously, it won't happen again," Gabe said. Pauling knew he believed himself, but she knew it wasn't true. In a day or two Gabe would forget it and go back to being his sexually frustrated self.

Back at the Nest, they said their good nights and Pauling went to her room, undressed and got into the shower. She felt woozy and unstable. She couldn't remember the last time she'd had so much to drink.

The hot water felt great and she let it pound onto her face and neck. Afterward, she toweled off, brushed her teeth and collapsed onto her bed. She hadn't learned a whole lot, but tomorrow morning she knew her head would recognize the effort.

As she closed her eyes, she thought of the graffiti she'd seen at Rag City.

PJ was here.

When had Paige been there? And with who? Gabe? And how often had she gone? Just the once, and the novelty of being there had inspired her to leave her mark?

There were plenty of questions and no answers.

It did make Pauling think, though. Janey had just said that Paige often didn't return home at night. And it had been made clear to Pauling that certain parts of the island were off-limits. So while it made perfect sense that a wannabe rebel like Gabe had sneaked into Rag City, it was somewhat surprising to Pauling that Paige had done the same thing.

It made her wonder how many other things about Paige she didn't know. Human beings weren't just people, they were unique collections of secrets.

In the morning she awoke with a surprisingly mild hangover. In the kitchen, she put some sugar in her coffee and carried the oversized mug back to her room.

She fired up the laptop and drank coffee while she waited.

Gabe must have made the coffee because it was strong as hell. She was glad she'd cut it with some sugar otherwise it would have been nearly undrinkable.

Immediately, she felt her blood start to pulse and the small headache was already gone.

Her screen had come to life and now she looked at the email Blake had sent her.

There were a ton of attachments he had put into a zip file. But his instructions were clear: immediately open the folder marked "Sirrine."

Pauling did as instructed.

She scanned the first few lines and leaned back in her chair.

"Holy shit," she whispered.

CHAPTER THIRTY-TWO

T he first thing Pauling saw was the headline of a newspaper clipping.

Respected Professor Forced to Resign Amid Sex Scandal Rumors

The article continued:

Renowned Ornithological Professor Dr. Abner Sirrine announced his resignation yesterday from California State College. School administrators were alerted to a sexual abuse complaint filed by one of Dr. Sirrine's students. Although investigators found the results inconclusive the administrators felt that due to the severe nature of the complaint, Dr. Sirrine should be forced to resign.

Pauling continued to read the background Blake had supplied. She set aside the scandalous stuff and went to a biography from one of Dr. Sirrine's earlier employers.

It told her that Abner had graduated from a prestigious private school on the East Coast and then went to Dartmouth where he graduated magna cum laude. He immediately began writing papers and gaining recognition for his insights into bird migrations, in particular the birds of southern California. These papers had ultimately led to his being offered the position at California State College, where he'd been an instructor for decades.

Pauling learned that after his resignation, Dr. Sirrine went off the grid before he reappeared for the Bird Conservatory. Pauling wondered if the reason he was accepted for the job was that he wouldn't have any underage females working for him.

That made sense to Pauling. She continued to read the material from Blake on Dr. Sirrine until she had completed nearly everything.

Before she dug into information on the others she thought about what she'd read.

Could it be that Dr. Sirrine had anything to do with Paige's death?

On the surface, it seemed absurd.

Dr. Sirrine was like a goofy old uncle. Additionally, his physicality was less than impressive. He didn't look fragile necessarily, but he certainly wasn't much of a physical specimen.

Pauling saw no way in which Dr. Sirrine could overpower Paige.

Unless of course Paige had been under the influence of something, knowingly or unknowingly. Pauling thought of her escapades the night before. But nothing she had seen in Dr. Abner Sirrine suggested he would've killed Paige.

But if there was one thing she had learned at the FBI, it was to never underestimate the potential for evil in the human heart.

CHAPTER THIRTY-THREE

After Pauling ate breakfast and had a couple more cups of coffee, she decided to skip the field trip Dr. Sirrine had planned for her and instead commandeered the jeep and drove it directly to the commander's office.

She parked in the little gravel parking lot outside a civilian-looking building that looked more a real estate agent's office than military headquarters.

Pauling walked inside and saw two offices. One was empty and the other was occupied by Commander Bill Wilkins and seated in a chair across from him, Michael Tallon.

Pauling decided to be bold and ignore protocol so she walked right up to the office and stood outside the doorway.

Wilkins looked at her and his expression made Michael Tallon turn and look over his shoulder. When he saw Pauling, he smiled.

"Hey! Pauling, how are you doing?"

"I'm doing fine. How are you? Hello, Bill."

"Pauling," Wilkins replied.

"Couldn't be better," Tallon answered. "Are you here to see me or this old salt?"

"The old salt," she said.

"No problem, we were just finishing up," Tallon said. "I'll talk to you later, Bill." Tallon got to his feet, nodded at her as he walked past and then stopped.

"Hey, have you ever gone diving for lobsters before?"

"No, can't say that I have," Pauling answered.

"Great. Let's do it. You can't come out to San Clemente and never go lobster diving. It's a rite of passage."

"Sounds interesting," Pauling said.

"I'll pick you up tomorrow morning."

He walked on and Pauling turned to Commander Wilkins.

"Is he serious?" she asked.

Wilkins nodded. "Yeah, I'm afraid so. I try not to eat too much lobster, as good as they are. High in cholesterol."

Pauling took the chair in which Tallon had been sitting.

"So what can I do for you?" Wilkins said.

"Well, you offered to give me a tour of your part of the island so I thought I would finally take you up on that," she said. "Or is now a bad time? Is this the kind of thing you schedule?"

"I did, in fact, have a couple things on today's calendar but when a beautiful woman like yourself offers to spend some time with me, I'm not gonna turn her down," Wilkins replied. "I may be old but I haven't lost my faculties."

He snatched up a set of keys and gestured for Pauling to follow him.

"So who actually provides law enforcement for the island?" she asked, knowing the answer but wanting to see what he would say. "Is it the military police or your own guys? Or is there an outside police force whose jurisdiction the island falls under?"

"You get right to the point, don't you?" he said, glancing

at Pauling. "Technically, we fall under the jurisdiction of the Los Angeles County Sheriff's Department whose nearest precinct is actually on Catalina Island. Have you ever been to Catalina Island?"

Pauling thought about it. "Yes, I have been on Catalina but it was a long time ago when I was a little girl."

Wilkins led her outside to a small blue pickup truck and he took the wheel. She slid into the passenger seat. The truck smelled like coffee and cigarettes.

"We're not a very big operation," he said. "We only have a couple hundred people here usually. Mostly guys rotating in for training and rotating out. The people who are here on a full-time basis tend to be the Seabees who are the construction people from the Navy. Of course the kitchen staff are year-round. The maintenance people are year-round, too."

Wilkins drove her from one end of the island to the other, pointing out the various locations of training sites. Most of them were not much to look at.

As they drove, she occasionally spotted groups of men jogging.

The tour took less than an hour and Pauling didn't see anything that surprised her, or that she hadn't seen before.

The most interesting thing to note was what Wilkins hadn't shown her.

Rag City.

Eventually, they wound up back at Wilkins' office.

"So were you shocked when the body of Paige Jones showed up?" she asked.

"Absolutely," he said casually, as if she'd asked him about the weather report. "We see training accidents all the time. Some of them are fatal. But the birdies? Nothing ever happens to them. It was a shame. I'd met her, saw her occasionally at the Crab. A beautiful girl."

Pauling nodded.

The phone on the desk rang. Pauling almost chuckled. Who had landlines anymore?

"You'll have to excuse me," he said.

"Thank you for the tour."

He nodded to her as he picked up the phone.

CHAPTER THIRTY-FOUR

She found Dr. Sirrine standing outside the herbarium. He was examining a new batch of seeds that had been collected that morning.

Pauling took in his appearance, which was the same as always. Khakis, a barn jacket, worn leather boat shoes and a field hat.

"Any exciting discoveries?" Pauling asked.

Dr. Sirrine shook his head.

"No, but it's been a dry season and the ground cover isn't doing as well as we'd hoped," he said. "But it's not horrible. Plenty of camouflage for our favorite birds' food."

"That's good," Pauling said. "Hey, do you have a minute? I'd like to talk to you about something."

Dr. Sirrine put down the seeds he'd been studying and glanced at her.

"This sounds serious."

Pauling didn't respond.

He pointed to a bench near the back of the building. They walked to it together and sat down.

"What did you want to discuss?" he asked.

"I've read the newspaper articles about your departure from California State College," Pauling began. "I guess I wanted to hear your side of the story."

Dr. Sirrine sighed and rubbed his hands on his thighs, brushing off some dirt and loose grass he'd collected during his research.

"What makes you possibly think I would want to talk about that?" he snapped. "It's ancient history."

"So do the newspaper stories tell the whole truth? Or is there more to the story?"

"Truth and reality are two different things," he explained, a tone of condescension in his voice. "They told their truth, and I have mine. The reality depends on which lens you're standing behind."

"Spoken like a true professor," Pauling said. She paused, and was amazed at how right at home she felt. She'd interrogated some bad people in her life. The naturalist sitting next to her was severely undermatched.

"How much does the Bird Conservatory know?" Pauling asked.

Pauling sensed Dr. Sirrine's back stiffen at the mention of it.

"Is that a threat?"

"I don't know," she answered. "Do you feel threatened by the idea of me talking to them? Or do they already know your full history?"

In other words, Pauling thought, *yes, it's a threat all right*.

Body language oftentimes speaks several volumes louder than verbal speech. When Dr. Sirrine's body seemed to fold in on itself, Pauling knew she had cracked him.

"There was nothing, absolutely nothing, untoward," he finally said. "The fact was, she had been my student, but wasn't under my tutelage when we began seeing one another. She was eighteen. I was thirty-eight."

A truck drove by on Perimeter Road and Dr. Sirrine waited for its sound to fade.

"I was lonely, she was in need of adventure. For a brief time, we found solace with each other."

His voice had warmed, and Pauling instinctively knew Dr. Sirrine still had feelings for the woman.

"But as is so often the case with these things, it ended badly," he explained. "For someone my age, I knew these things happened. She was young, and didn't know how to handle it, so she lied and said the relationship had begun six months before it actually did. When she was seventeen. She knew what would happen to me. And it did."

"Did she ever recant her story?" Pauling asked.

Dr. Sirrine shook his head. "No, she changed her story, repeatedly. But she never recanted the fictional start date. However, each time she told the story she added in new details, mostly regarding my depravity. It was almost like she felt she couldn't tell the same story over and over. She needed to spice it up each time. Needless to say, the damage to my teaching career was irrevocable."

Pauling leaned back against the bench. She folded her arms across her chest.

"What did you think when they found Paige's body?"

His laugh was full of cynicism. "I naturally thought of myself. I figured someone would eventually come calling, questioning me regarding my whereabouts, that kind of thing. I figured it would be the police."

"And did they?"

"They talked to me about her, but I had nothing to tell them. And they only asked about her in the context of a drowning. They clearly felt foul play wasn't involved, and frankly, I felt the same way. That is, until you arrived. And then I began to wonder who had hired an investigator, and why."

Pauling ignored the bait.

"Did they ask about your past?" she asked.

"No."

He looked directly at her.

"You're the first."

CHAPTER THIRTY-FIVE

When Pauling was finished talking with Dr. Sirrine and he had gone back to the Nest, she heard movement behind her and a door banged shut. She got up from the bench and walked around to where she heard the sound. There was a door that must have been a side entrance to the herbarium.

Pauling went inside and Janey was standing at a rolling table, working with some soil samples.

Pauling wondered if Janey had been trying to listen in on her conversation with Dr. Sirrine.

And if so, why?

"Do you enjoy your work here?" Pauling asked, as she walked up to watch Janey.

Janey spoke quickly, almost nervously. "I enjoy what I do, but not much else. You know, when I came here a lot of people at the Bird Conservatory said the work was rewarding but you'll live in isolation. There's nothing to do there, they said. You'll lose contact with friends and family and being able to do social things. And I found out they were right."

It had all come out in a gushing torrent and Pauling

suspected Janey had been listening to her conversation with Dr. Sirrine. She'd been a little too eager to fill the void.

"But you do enjoy the work?" Pauling asked. "Are you achieving things professionally?"

Janey stopped what she was doing and turned to Pauling, almost as if she hadn't fully realized she was there until that moment.

"Do *you* enjoy what *you're* doing?" Janey asked. Her tone was verging on anger. Pauling was surprised. What had she done to piss off this woman?

"Are you achieving things that you want to achieve in a professional sense?" Janey persisted. Some of the snark had gone out of her tone, but Pauling sensed there was a lot of emotion behind the question.

Pauling knew what Janey was getting at. She was obviously thinking that Pauling was snooping around about Paige's death. *But why would that upset her?*

"I find my work challenging," Pauling said. "But I feel that what I do is very important."

Pauling followed Janey as she carried a tray of seedlings and put it under a grow light.

"I wanted to thank you for telling me about Paige and some of her habits," Pauling tried, softening her tone as much as possible. "I was wondering, was there anything else you can think of? Anything else that happened to Paige while she was out here? Anyone who might've wanted to hurt her?"

Janey frowned. "No. I did remember one thing though, and I meant to tell you. One morning I saw Paige at breakfast and her face was puffy and red and there were marks on her throat. It was hard to tell what they were though. There are a lot of strange pollens out here and sometimes we have allergic reactions. Not to mention all kinds of spiders and flies and mosquitoes. We're constantly getting bitten," Janey said. "But there was a part of me that wondered if someone had slapped her around a little bit. Maybe even put their hands around her throat. Then again, I figured I might have been paranoid or something. And it wasn't my place to ask."

"So you didn't ask her about the marks?" Pauling asked.

"Not right away, but eventually I sort of did. A couple of times. But she never wanted to talk about them, and she never told me what happened. As far as I know she never told anyone."

Janey set down the tray of soil as if it was a punctuation mark on what she said. And then she walked away.

CHAPTER THIRTY-SIX

P auling spent a fitful evening going over the material
Blake had sent her, updating her dossiers on
everyone involved and then eventually falling asleep.

She had a bad night's sleep punctuated by a nightmare in
which she was stranded in the desert facing a pickup truck
with a huge machine gun installed in the truck bed, manned
by a terrorist.

When she awoke, she got her coffee and found Michael
Tallon waiting for her.

She'd forgotten about his offer to take her diving for
lobster.

"Ever had lobster for breakfast?" he asked. His blue eyes
shone like beacons and Pauling realized once again how
incredibly good-looking he was. And then she caught herself.
She was here to investigate Paige's death. Not to meet a
handsome military guy.

She wasn't sure why she had accepted the offer in the first
place. But it occurred to her that Paige's journal had refer-
enced a man with blue eyes. And Paige had washed up on the
shore as if she'd been out swimming.

So when a man with blue eyes invited her out for a diving expedition she felt, as an investigator, she had to say yes.

Because in the back of her mind, she couldn't help but wonder if this was exactly how Paige had met her unfortunate demise.

An innocent offer from Michael Tallon.

Pauling didn't think it would be the case, but she also felt like she needed some insurance.

Besides, she still had no idea if Paige's poem was even about Michael Tallon, or if it was about a man at all. It all depended upon the interpretation.

Before she left, Pauling sent an email to Blake, letting him know that she was going out on a dive boat with a Michael Tallon. She made it sound like a casual mention in a frivolous email and refrained from specifically asking Blake to do anything.

Pauling also made a concerted effort not to mention how angry she felt that Jack Reacher was nowhere to be found. Nathan Jones would have to give her a proper explanation when she got back.

They took Perimeter Road down to the military's ship-yard. There were some boats with machine guns on them and Pauling was again reminded of her dream.

"Those are called RHIBS," Tallon explained. "Rigid Hull Inflatable Boats."

He pointed over toward another set of two boats that were bigger and held more machine guns. "Those are called Mark Vs."

Tallon parked the vehicle and they made their way down to the pier where Tallon led her to a boat that looked like a glorified barge.

"Yeah, this isn't as sexy as those other boats but it'll get the job done," he said. "This is our backup boat for dive training. Right now there's hardly anything on it which makes it perfect for us to go look for some lobster."

It was a small vessel maybe 25 feet in length but at least 15 feet wide. There was a little pilothouse and then there were rows of oxygen tanks on the side along with dive gear.

"Why don't you untie us while I fire up the engines?" he said.

"Aye aye, captain," she said.

Pauling went to the bow and stern of the boat and undid the thick ropes holding the barge in place as she heard the rumble of what she assumed to be a big diesel engine get going.

They slowly pulled out of the harbor and into an immediate chop. The barge didn't exactly rise and fall with the waves as much as plow through them, occasionally bumping and going sideways.

Pauling made no move to put on a life jacket, nor did Tallon. Of course, for all she knew, Tallon could have been a Navy SEAL. His Ball watch, the NEDU, meant Navy Experimental Dive Unit. Maybe there was more to that story than he'd indicated.

"The best place is about a mile out. There's some structure and the season's right."

He had come out of the pilothouse, leaving the barge on some sort of autopilot, she guessed.

"Have you done any diving?" he asked.

"A little," she said. "I was certified once awhile back on a Caribbean vacation."

"Well, the good thing is the water clarity out here is fantastic, so it shouldn't be much of a problem."

He gave her a wet suit and they geared up.

"What about the sharks?" she asked.

Pauling still hadn't decided if she was going to do this or not. A lot of it depended on Tallon's answer.

"They won't bother you," he said. "It's the middle of the day and I've done this a thousand times. Now, if it was midnight, no, I wouldn't be doing this."

Not exactly what she wanted to hear, but at least he sounded honest.

They pulled out into the open ocean and occasionally Pauling glanced back at San Clemente. It already looked so small, she found it hard to believe she was living on it temporarily.

Ahead, there was a large stone outcropping with a strange white cap. There were thousands of birds on the rock, or in the air above it.

"Bird Shit Rock," Tallon said.

"Lovely," Pauling replied.

By the time they got most of the gear ready, Tallon glanced up and said, "Great, we're here."

He shut the engines off and somewhere an anchor splashed into the water.

They did tests for each other's air and then dropped into the sea.

Pauling was fascinated with the color of the water. And she was also terrified of the sharks she'd seen.

Tallon led the way, swimming down to a structure covered in green. Pauling noticed Tallon had some sort of large glove on his hand.

Suddenly, a lobster shot out of the structure and Tallon caught him expertly with the glove. He stuffed it into a bag on the side of his hip.

He gestured toward Pauling and gave her the glove. She slipped it on, realizing it was some sort of hockey goalie's glove.

A lobster scooted out in front of her and she grabbed it with the glove, but it squirted out from her grasp and got away. She repeated this several times.

Tallon made a gesture to her that looked like he was saying she needed to squeeze harder.

The next lobster that came she did just that and this time, it stayed in the glove.

Tallon slid it into his bag and she gave him the glove back. She had caught one. That was good enough for her.

Pauling watched while Tallon caught a few more lobsters and then she was startled when a sea lion zipped between them, going for Tallon's lobster catch.

He was able to maneuver quickly enough to avoid the thief.

They surfaced and climbed back onto the barge.

"Well done, Pauling," he said.

"Thanks, you were pretty handy with that hockey glove. Although that sea lion almost had an easy feast."

"Yeah, it's sort of a game with them. Sometimes I'll feed them a couple for their troubles."

Pauling stripped out of her gear and helped Tallon stow the lobsters in a cooler filled with ice.

Tallon pulled a couple bottles of beer from another cooler she hadn't even noticed.

They sat on the end of the barge, the warm sun blasting down on them and the chill she'd felt from the water quickly went away.

She felt warm, safe and the beer was perfect.

They clinked bottles.

"To fresh lobster," Pauling said.

"And good company."

CHAPTER THIRTY-SEVEN

"You in the mood for a burger?" Ted asked her when she came back to the Nest after her lobster-diving expedition. By now, it was early evening and Pauling was tired from her day on the water.

She was still thinking about Michael Tallon and what Janey had told her about Paige.

"A burger?" she asked.

"Yeah, at the Crab," Ted said. His mop of black hair was hanging over his eyes and Pauling had a negative reply on the tip of her tongue.

But she bit it back. She and Michael had grilled the lobsters on the boat and had them for lunch and she wasn't really hungry.

"Sure," she said. "I just need a couple of minutes first, is that okay?"

"Yeah, I'll grab a beer while I wait."

Pauling went back to her room and quickly changed her clothes.

Something told her this was going to be different than her

outing with Gabe. Gabe wore his heart on his sleeve and was consumed with lust.

Ted was quiet. Bookish, almost.

She joined him in a white jeep and they drove to the Salty Crab.

Pauling was beginning to wonder how many more times she would have to go to the bar.

But she wasn't ready to completely write off the Crab just yet; besides, getting people to drink tended to help an investigation. The drunk man's tongue speaks the sober man's mind, right?

Ted parked and they went inside.

Pauling also understood the sensory deprivation that naturally occurs on San Clemente Island. It has to. There are no shopping malls. No row of restaurants. No residential neighborhoods with kids playing in the yard. All there is on the island is a foreign landscape, nearly completely devoid of trees, and beyond it, ocean.

The Crab served a useful purpose. Seeing other human beings, talking to them.

And fried food.

They got a table near the kitchen, both ordered cheeseburgers with french fries.

Pauling already felt vaguely ill. She hadn't had a salad since her lunch with Tallon and her diet had become a steady supply of meat and carbs. And booze.

Her mind briefly drifted back to Michael Tallon. She wondered where he was and what he was doing.

"Christ, I'm so hungry," Ted said. The food was delivered in red plastic baskets. Again, it reminded Pauling of greasy spoons back in the day.

Pauling ate her burger and had to agree with Ted, it was good. But she couldn't eat like this much longer.

Someone bumped into her from behind.

Pauling turned and looked into the sweaty, greasy face of a woman. At first, she thought it was a man. But when the woman looked down at her and said, "Fuck outta my way," Pauling could tell it was a woman.

Her arms were huge, and one of them sported a barbed wire tattoo around the impressive bicep.

The woman sat down a few tables away from Pauling and Ted.

"Uh-oh," Ted said.

Pauling and Ted tried to focus on their cheeseburgers. Pauling's was only half-eaten. Ted had demolished his but was picking at his fries. Pauling drank some of her beer when a shadow fell across the table. She looked up and saw the woman who had bumped into her staring down at her.

"Who the hell are you?" the woman asked. Pauling could smell the alcohol on her breath and her pupils were totally dilated. She was clearly drunk.

"My name is Pauling. What's yours?"

"Oh great, another little birdie to fly around and bug the shit out of me," the woman said, ignoring Pauling's question.

"Look, we're just trying to have some cheeseburgers and a beer and then we're gonna get out of here," Ted said. "No need for any problem here."

"You goddamn right there's not gonna be a problem," the woman said, her voice thick and slurry. "In the future, you bitches stay away from me."

She left and went back to her table. There was a guy at her table. He was big with a bulging pot belly and a dirty t-shirt.

"I think those are the construction people," Ted said. "They tend to be kind of rough. A lot of times they're worse than the military guys."

"Yeah, why did she have such a problem with me?" Pauling said.

"Because you're competition," Ted said. "I have a feeling that when the guys are drunk, even on this island where there's hardly any women and the guys are all horny, she probably still has problems getting laid."

"Shocking with that winning personality of hers," Pauling said.

"And look at her," Ted said, glancing over Pauling's shoulder.

"I'd rather not."

"What you lookin' at?" The man with the big gut stood up and pointed at Ted.

"Holy shit," Ted said.

The man's chair scraped across the floor.

"Hey, come on guys!" a voice called from another table. A man stood and Pauling recognized him as the pilot from the plane that brought her out to the island. He was sitting with his co-pilot and a military guy she hadn't seen before.

"Give me a round for that table!" he shouted at the bartender and then walked over to Pauling's table. He stuck out his hand.

"Brock Jamison, I flew you out here. Along with my partner over there, Josh Troyer."

He nodded at the table with the construction couple, who'd suddenly gone quiet.

"It's kind of like that Asian philosophy of how if you save someone's life you're responsible for them," Jamison said. "That's how I see it. When I fly you out here, my job isn't over."

He laughed and Pauling was glad he was there. She and Ted were probably no match for those two.

"Come on, Jamison, quit trying to be a hero," Troyer said, and approached the table. "It doesn't suit you very well."

He looked at Pauling. "I remember you. Didn't we just fly

out here a couple days ago? And you're causing problems already?" He winked at her.

Brock Jamison had returned from the bar with a tray of tequila shots. He took them over to the construction workers' table and they spoke quietly.

Pauling glanced over and they were looking at her, scowling. But the big guy had sat back down.

Jamison returned to their table.

"You can either come and sit with us or you've probably got about ten minutes before those new shots of tequila wear off and they start looking for a fight again."

Ted stood. "I think we're going to go," he said.

Pauling decided not to push her luck.

"Thank you for that," she said to Jamison and nodded her head toward the loud-mouthed drunkards.

"My pleasure," he said.

Pauling and Ted headed for the door. As they veered wide around the construction workers' table the woman looked up at Pauling.

"Watch it, birdie or you'll fly away forever."

CHAPTER THIRTY-EIGHT

Pauling decided to go for a walk, although it wasn't really possible to go for a true, aimless walk. Not unless you wanted to get shot by a sniper or step on a land mine.

No, she had to settle for walking around the birders' compound.

She said good night to Ted and walked around behind the main building. The cheeseburger, even though she'd eaten only half of it due to the interruption by the manly female construction worker, sat heavy in her stomach.

When she got off this island, she was going to eat nothing but salads of mixed greens for a month straight. And plenty of green tea. Plus, she would work out every damn day. Hardcore.

She walked under a sky filled with stars, an absolutely windless night and the sound of the surf pounding below. As she walked, she thought about Paige.

The first image that came to mind was that of Paige getting her ass kicked by the woman Pauling had just met at the Salty Crab. She made a note to find out who the woman was, her name, and talk to her, preferably when the woman wasn't drunk and belligerent. She didn't know if the woman was never *not* drunk or belligerent, but she would find out.

She walked past the herbarium, past the maintenance shed with the trucks and the gas pumps. The road sloped down and she followed it, careful not to re-emerge onto the road. That was definitely not the place to be. Here, on the south side of the complex, she knew the military generally didn't train.

However, she had no intention of taking a chance.

In the distance, she heard the high-pitched howl of what she assumed was a fox. They had once been extremely prevalent on the island, but had seen their numbers dwindle over the years. The population was stable, though, and in no danger of extinction.

Pauling walked on, wanting to walk faster but aware that she had a limited range of travel. She would have to do laps–

Slap.

She stopped in her tracks.

The sound of something hitting flesh. It sounded like a hand. Like someone had slapped someone's face.

She waited.

Slap.

It was to her left. Past the maintenance buildings, toward a tiny shed used for storage. Now, she saw a small light visible only from this side of the building.

She walked toward it, careful not to make a sound.

Slap.

Pauling walked ahead, her ears straining for any voices.

In the corner of her vision, just around the edge of the tiny shed, she saw a foot. Its laces were pressed into the ground, as if the owner was kneeling.

Pauling widened her approach, and the scene came into view.

Dr. Sirrine was on his knees behind Janey, his pants down and his naked ass exposed to the moon.

Janey's lower half was naked, her buttocks visible as Dr. Sirrine thrust into her and slapped her naked ass.

Pauling stood, frozen.

"You like that, don't you?" Dr. Sirrine said, his voice a growl.

"Yes, harder," Janey said.

Pauling had seen enough.

She turned and tripped over a discarded set of plumbing pipes. She fell on her face in the long grass.

Pauling heard the sound of feet scraping in the dirt and the rattle of a belt buckle. She ran toward the Nest, ducking around the larger maintenance building and then beelining it for the Nest.

She made it inside and hurried to her room, let herself in and shut the door.

She left the light off.

It was a strange sense of guilt, but she simply didn't want Dr. Sirrine and Janey to know that she had seen them. But it made her head spin. She'd figured there would be some cases of romance between the men and women who worked at the Nest, but she never would have figured on Dr. Sirrine and Janey. The age difference. The personalities.

But most importantly, she wondered how it affected her investigation of what happened with Paige.

Had Dr. Sirrine, who made every effort to appear morally superior, made advances on Paige? He'd clearly made them, and succeeded, with Janey.

There was no way Paige would have acquiesced to Dr. Sirrine.

But again, Pauling knew when it came to human beings, one could never really be sure of anything.

CHAPTER THIRTY-NINE

In the morning, Pauling grabbed a cup of coffee and the keys to one of the pickup trucks.

She no longer felt the need to ask. As she drove, she thought about island fever, that feeling of claustrophobia some people succumbed to. She wasn't there yet, but the sense of isolation was strong.

Now, she drove ahead past the cafeteria building and around the administration building to where she'd been told by Gabe the maintenance staff was housed.

The maintenance department most likely included the construction workers.

Pauling smiled at the idea of waking up the construction woman from the night before. It would be great payback for the woman's boorish behavior. Pauling hoped she was hungover and feeling terrible.

She would have some fun with it, she decided.

There was an open two-story aluminum-sided garage set back from a driveway with a sign that read "Maintenance."

Pauling pulled the truck into the driveway, parked it and went inside.

The smell of diesel fuel was strong, and she heard the clang of metal.

There appeared to be no one in the front half of the garage. She walked toward the back, eventually seeing a desk with an ancient computer sitting on top of it.

Her friend from the bar was sprawled on a couch that had been pushed up against the wall.

Her face was pale and she had a Gatorade in her hand.

She looked up at Pauling. Her bloodshot eyes narrowed.

"What do you want?" she asked.

"I'd like to talk to you."

The woman shook her head.

"I've got nothing to say," she said, her voice sounding like sandpaper. "If I said something last night you don't like, go ahead and complain to my supervisor."

The guy from the Crab with the pot belly and dirty t-shirt stepped into the space from a doorway off to the left. He still had on the same shirt.

"There he is now," the woman said.

He had a giant iron wrench in his hand.

Pauling smiled.

"No complaints about last night," Pauling said. "I had fun. I actually wanted to ask you about Paige Jones. She worked with the Bird Conservatory here."

"She the dead girl?"

"What's your name, by the way?" Pauling asked.

"I'm Deb. And no, I don't remember her."

"Shit, you don't remember anything," the guy said.

"What's your name?" Pauling asked him.

"The hell should I tell you?" he said. His eyebrow was raised and he was hefting the wrench with apparent pleasure.

"Why not?" Pauling answered.

He nodded as if that was a good enough response for him. "I'm Donnie. I don't remember her, but I heard one of the birdies died. Was that her? And that's why you're asking around?"

"Paige was a very beautiful girl, dark hair." Pauling produced the photo of Paige that she'd brought along.

"Shit yeah, I remember her," Donnie said. "Great ass. Those military guys ate her up."

"Literally," Deb said. She and Donnie high-fived.

"Did you ever threaten her like you did me?" Pauling asked.

Donnie dropped his hands by his side like he was about to brawl. Deb's head popped up and she winced, as if the movement hurt her.

"Probably," Deb said. "But I sure didn't kill her if that's what you're asking. Christ. The booze sometimes makes me shoot my mouth off, that's all."

"Any idea who might have wanted to hurt her?" Pauling asked.

"Hurt her? I thought the dumb bitch drowned," Donnie said.

"What a touching eulogy," Pauling said. "Answer the question. Was anyone after her?"

"Hell, all those guys were after her," Deb said, sorrow and disappointment audible in her voice. "Maybe she screwed one of them over. They all got fragile egos."

"Big egos and little dicks," Donnie said, puffing himself up and looking at Pauling.

"How would you know?" Deb asked.

She and Pauling looked at Donnie.

"Piss off, both of you," he said and walked back out the door. Deb laid back on the couch and put a towel over her face.

"Fly away, birdie," she said.

CHAPTER FORTY

auling got back into the pickup truck, pulled out into the driveway and made it to the intersection with Perimeter Road, next to the maintenance sign.

Another car drove by and behind the wheel she saw Michael Tallon. His face registered no surprise but he hit the brakes hard and nearly skidded to a stop. He put his car in reverse and backed up in front of her. Pauling pulled out onto the road so they were side by side. She rolled down her window and he did the same.

"What are you doing out here?" he asked.

"Oh, I was just looking to see if they needed a full-time mechanic. You know I'm a real grease monkey."

"Hmm, I didn't realize that. Wait here," he said. He pulled his car off onto the shoulder, put the hazard lights on and ran around to the side of her pickup. He opened the door and hopped into her passenger seat.

Pauling put the truck in gear and pulled off onto the shoulder.

"I've been meaning to ask," Tallon said. "What is it you do with the bird people again?"

She drummed her fingers on the steering wheel. "Why?"

He shrugged his shoulders. "I seem to recall you telling me you had something to do with computers."

"Yeah, I believe I said something like that," she said. Pauling wondered where this was coming from. He hadn't asked her any of these kinds of questions when they'd gone diving. Maybe he hadn't wanted to spoil the outing.

He furrowed his brow as if he was trying to reconcile that idea.

"It just seems like you remind me of a certain kind of person," he said.

"Oh yeah, what kind of person is that?"

"Well, you know I did a lot of work in Special Ops," he grinned at her. "Still do, occasionally, maybe."

Pauling knew that was the case, she'd guessed that the minute she'd met him.

"We did a lot of missions all over the world and I worked with a lot of different people," he continued. "You don't seem like a boots-on-the-ground kind of person, too much. But you do remind me of some people I worked with. There were a few folks who helped plan strategy, you know, more of an analysis kind of thing. You remind me of them. I don't know, it's just a feeling.

Pauling wondered if he knew who she really was, because he had described what she'd done at the FBI. And was he asking her this because he already knew it to be true? Had they dug into classified files and found out who she really was?

For a brief moment Pauling thought about telling him the truth. But then she changed her mind.

"Don't you have somewhere you need to be?" she asked, a bit abruptly.

Tallon laughed, opened the door and got out of the truck.

He leaned on the doorframe and looked at Pauling. "Maybe one day you'll tell me who you really are." He tapped the roof twice and walked back to his car.

Pauling drove away.

He's right, she thought. One day I probably will.

CHAPTER FORTY-ONE

Pauling drove back to the Nest and saw Ted unloading a bunch of gear from the back of his truck. She parked, went over and lent him a hand. There were cardboard boxes of various shapes and sizes, some heavy, some light.

"What's in this?"

"Mostly supplies," he said. Pauling grabbed a box and followed Ted around to the back of the building and started stacking the boxes near a table.

They went back and forth making trips from the truck to the stack and it took them nearly half an hour to completely unload the vehicle's cargo.

"Did these just come in on the plane today?"

"Yep," Ted said.

They finished and sat down at the table. "That was a good workout," Pauling said. Ted grabbed them each a bottled water from somewhere.

"So Ted, how well did you know Paige?"

"Give me a break," Ted said, his even demeanor dropping and going right into Angry Ted.

"You know, I know you're asking everybody about this and I know you're going around trying to find a bunch of stuff out. Why don't you just leave the dead alone? If you aren't going to, at least just leave me alone about it, okay?"

Ted's face had gotten red and Pauling knew it wasn't from the exertion of unloading the gear. "I had nothing to do with anything related to Paige. Okay? I hardly knew her, I barely even talked to her. She went out every night. She had a lot of boyfriends and I'm not judging. But you don't have to investigate me if that's what you're doing."

"I'm not investigating you," Pauling answered evenly. "I'm just wondering if you knew anything about her."

Ted snorted. "Oh bullshit, Pauling. We've all talked about you and we all know you're not remotely involved with computers or anything else. So just give me a break, okay?"

It had all come out like a torrent and Pauling watched as Ted caught his breath and took a drink of his bottled water.

"You seem very emotional about this, Ted," she said, her voice calm and controlled. "I'm actually not an investigator, but I do believe when you find somebody who adamantly doesn't want to talk about something usually there is more to the story."

He slammed his bottled water down and it spilled onto the table.

"Enough with the psychobabble! Jesus Christ!" he thundered at her. "Thanks for helping me with the boxes. Now just leave me alone, okay?"

He stormed off out of the building.

Pauling grabbed her water and tried to figure out why Ted was suddenly so emotional about her questions.

Something he had said struck her.

Leave the dead alone.

It suddenly gave her an idea and she realized she should have done it already.

CHAPTER FORTY-TWO

Back in her room Pauling fired up her laptop. She sent a message to Blake asking him if he could hack into the Los Angeles County Sheriff's Department website and track down the autopsy records for Paige Jones.

There had been a note in the paperwork Nathan had given Pauling regarding how an autopsy had been performed but that it had been inadequate to the state of the remains. But now Pauling wondered if an autopsy had at least been attempted, maybe they'd recorded something. Anything would be helpful at this point.

It might have seemed a strange request to ask Blake to hack the LASD, but Pauling knew Blake had once hacked into another law enforcement website and that one was linked to the federal government.

So she figured getting into a much smaller organization should be easier.

Pauling also remembered that Dr. Sirrine had set up the afternoon for her to go into the field with Ted.

Oh, that should be fun, she thought. Pauling figured Ted would take one look at her and cancel the outing.

It didn't matter because Pauling didn't want to spend the afternoon with Ted. She realized instead that she really needed to go and speak to the investigator who had overseen the examination of Paige upon the discovery of her body. According to Commander Wilkins, the investigating authority was on Catalina Island.

Pauling thought about how she could get there.

She knew there weren't flights to the island. She knew she just couldn't catch a ferry there, either. All transportation to and from San Clemente Island had to be sanctioned by the military.

What you really needed was a friend with a boat.

A small smile crept onto her face. Michael had given her his cell phone number and told her that the military had a small tower on the island which let people call each other on San Clemente, but that it wasn't strong enough to reach people on the mainland.

Pauling sent a text message to Michael asking him if he'd ever been to Catalina Island.

He texted back right away. *Sure. Have you?*

A long time ago.

He wrote back: *Weather is supposed to be great tomorrow. Low winds. We could grab a boat and go.*

She accepted the invitation she had forced, and then put her phone down. Back on the laptop, she went onto the Los Angeles County Sheriff's Department website. Under the administrative section of the website Pauling found the detective in charge. She emailed him asking him if she could talk to him tomorrow and she included her cell phone.

The next morning, Tallon came and picked her up in the truck and they went down to the marina. He had authorized a boat that had been civilianized, meaning all of the weapons had been taken off and it was mostly used as a transport vessel.

They set out from San Clemente Island and it took them an hour to get to Catalina. They pulled into the harbor and found a spot to tie off the boat.

"What do you want to do first?" Tallon asked her.

"I'm starving. How about we get some food?"

They found a restaurant that was perched over the water with fantastic views of the hundreds of sailboats anchored. It really was a beautiful harbor with the hills surrounding the water, and the community itself cascading down the hills settling on the water's edge.

Picture-postcard.

During lunch, Tallon talked about the rich history of Los Angeles celebrities coming out to Catalina Island for weekends of debauchery. Pauling was pretty sure she knew what he was getting at.

She feigned deep interest in her grilled shrimp salad.

After lunch Pauling said to Tallon, "Why don't you go off and explore on your own, while I do some shopping? We can rendezvous for drinks at happy hour."

He smiled at her. "If you want to get rid of me for a couple hours all you have to do is say so," he answered.

She gave him a kiss on the lips for an answer and it tasted good.

CHAPTER FORTY-THREE

P auling turned and walked up the hill leading to Main Street.

She found a little office for the sheriff's department and went inside.

"Is Officer Johnston here?" she asked. The guy looked up at her.

"He's at lunch." The man's eyes slid over to the clock and Pauling saw that he noticed it was 2:30 in the afternoon.

"He should be back anytime now," he added.

There was a seat across from the reception desk and Pauling sat. The guy at the desk looked at her and then turned in his chair. Pauling knew he was texting Johnston to let him know that he had a visitor.

Pauling looked around the space. It was a cross between a tourism office and a cop shop. There was a dolphin on the wall with the letters LASD across its side. Another wall showed photos of the harbor and next to them were a pair of shotguns locked into a rack.

The windows were open and Pauling saw no sign of air conditioning. She could smell the ocean.

Ten minutes later Officer Johnston walked in. He was a slim black man and he glanced down at Pauling.

"Are you Lauren Pauling?" he asked.

"I am."

"Paul Johnston," he said. "I got your email, come on back."

Pauling followed him to his office and they both sat down.

"So you wanted to ask me about Paige Jones?" he said.

"Yep, I sure did."

"Why would I want to help you?" Johnston asked, his tone easy and relaxed, in contrast to the nature of his question.

"Why wouldn't you?" she responded. "Don't you want to find out what happened to her? Are you totally convinced it was a drowning?"

Johnston's face remained blank. Pauling figured he was probably a pretty good poker player. He dug out a folder from a file cabinet, flipped it open, read for a bit, then snapped it shut.

"Look, we're what you would call a kind of satellite office," he said. "We got the call to liaison with the military guys. The remains were sent to the lab. And the results came back indicating death by drowning, followed by a shark attack. So the case was closed."

Pauling started to ask a question but he held up his hand.

"I spend most of my day dealing with drunks, shoplifters and two-bit drug dealers, mostly weed. And people just ripping off the tourists here. My bosses are back in Los Angeles. If you've got a problem with the way it was handled or just don't like the results, I suggest you take it up with them."

He swiveled in his chair and put the folder back in his file cabinet.

"That's it?" Pauling asked.

"Yes. Now kindly leave my office and let me take care of

Catalina Island. If you've got some kind of crazy ass conspiracy theory, take it up with my supervisors back on the mainland."

He stood and Pauling walked out of his office.

She emerged on the street and was dazzled by the bright sun and the reflections off the water.

Pauling knew she was making progress.

Johnston's overheated performance was just that, an act.

He knew more than he wanted to admit.

CHAPTER FORTY-FOUR

She and Michael decided to spend the night on Catalina Island. Pauling knew it was probably a ploy just to get her into bed, but she also realized that she didn't really have a problem with that plan.

They ate at a restaurant on the square. She chose a big salad with grilled vegetables. She figured it was a chance to add some greens to her diet that had largely been missing since her time on San Clemente.

Tallon got a grilled swordfish steak.

"How did your afternoon go?" he asked, a smile on his face, and a little gleam in his blue eyes. Pauling suspected he knew pretty much what she was doing.

"Oh, you know, a lot of stuff is so overpriced out here, but I found a few things."

"Meet anyone interesting?" he persisted. "Have any good conversations?"

She nearly smiled, but also knew that Tallon was still very much a suspect, even though her intuition was telling her he wasn't.

"You know how it goes, I'm sure," she answered.

"What do you mean?"

"There are people who love to talk and there are people who love to have their little secrets," she said and met him with a direct stare until he looked away.

She left it at that and he didn't pressure her for more information.

They went to a bar and had a few drinks and soon she felt a little drunk. At one point, he got her onto a dance floor and they did some kind of butchered cha cha.

They left and went to the hotel.

"Do you want to come up to my room for a little bit?" Tallon asked her.

"A little bit?" she asked.

"It's just an expression," he said.

"I appreciate the offer but I'm tired and a little too loopy to make that decision right now." The truth was, she was thinking of Paige and wondering if she'd been in this same position.

She gave him a kiss on the cheek and went to her room.

Alone.

CHAPTER FORTY-FIVE

They left early in the morning while the sea was calm and made it back to San Clemente quickly. Pauling didn't say much on the short trip back and neither did Tallon.

They docked the boat and Tallon dropped her back at the Nest where Pauling found an envelope that had been slid under her door.

It simply said: *Rag City. Ten o'clock tonight. I know what happened to Paige.*

There was no signature.

She spent the day reading through the files Blake had sent her. She'd already read them through several times, but she went through all of them, looking for things that she might have missed and adding thoughts and observations to her dossier.

But nothing jumped out at her.

The Dr. Sirrine/Janey angle was interesting but she couldn't help but feel it had nothing to do with Paige. Still, she couldn't rule it out.

By the time she was done updating her documents, it was

late afternoon and she realized she was exhausted. She laid on her bed, closed her eyes and napped.

When she awoke, it was night and she had an hour before her rendezvous with her mysterious source at Rag City.

She thought about precautions. She had no gun. No weapon of any kind. She considered calling Tallon and having him serve as backup, but she didn't want to do that.

Finally, she decided to send Blake an email so that at least one person on Earth knew where she was.

When the time came, she commandeered one of the trucks and made her way to Rag City. It took her longer than she'd expected, until she realized that the only time she'd been there before was when she was both high and a little bit drunk. After a half-dozen wrong turns, she finally found the place.

She parked and waited.

The note hadn't said where to meet. For some reason, she felt safer in the truck.

She waited, and ten o'clock came and went, and then ten-thirty. Pauling debated about driving back to the Nest.

But then a text message appeared on her phone from a blocked caller.

Come to the Town Square, in the apartment building. Don't worry, you are safe.

Yeah, right, Pauling thought. She also wondered, how did the person know that she was aware of Rag City? Gabe was the only person who knew she'd been there.

Unless someone had been watching her.

Well, she wasn't going to back out now.

She got out of the truck and walked into the middle of Rag City.

Pauling remembered the basic layout, and soon made her way to the structure that was meant to resemble an apartment building in the middle of Baghdad.

She stepped from the street up to the sidewalk, but she forgot about how much higher it was than in real life and stumbled. She fell to one knee and the cement wall where her head had been exploded, raining chunks of rock and dust down onto her.

She rolled forward and dove inside the building as another rifle shot tore up dirt in the street where she'd just been.

Inside the building, behind the wall, more shots punched through the cement.

It was a big rifle, Pauling realized. Maybe a high-powered sniper rifle like a Barrett. The kind that chambered a .50 caliber bullet.

In a flash, Pauling realized what a horrible situation she was in. Trapped inside a building at night with most likely a Special Ops sniper targeting her.

And she had no weapon.

CHAPTER FORTY-SIX

She was well and truly screwed.

Pauling knew firsthand the kind of equipment Special Ops snipers employed. Night vision goggles. Infrared. Scopes that could see the hair on a gnat's ass from a thousand yards.

She was in a world of trouble and cursed herself for not being better prepared.

Stop it, she told herself.

Make a plan.

The first thing she did was to get lower on the ground. Even the best scopes and night vision couldn't see through cement walls like the ones that were surrounding her.

It was her guess that the sniper had already started to move to a new location, maybe even coming into the building. If that happened and she was here, there was almost no way out.

So she had to move.

Pauling belly crawled across the floor toward the back of the room hoping there was some sort of backdoor and that the sniper wasn't going to be coming in that way.

Would she even be able to hear him?

Those guys moved in total silence. Still, she knew that the ground outside consisted at least partly of gravel and dirt. Which made for at least a slight possibility that the shooter might make some noise.

So she stayed still and listened.

Nothing.

And then, she heard the softest whisper of sound. Not a footstep. Certainly not on gravel.

It had sounded like fabric.

The quiet whisper of fabric on fabric. It had come from the front of the building.

Pauling raised herself up on her hands and knees and crawled toward the barely discernible window of darkness in the rear corner of the building that she hoped and prayed was a doorway.

She made her way to it.

Pauling continued forward and then one of her hands went past the floor and she fell out of the building. She landed on the ground and it was solid packed dirt. Luckily there was no sound as she slid all the way out of the building onto the ground outside and crawled so she wouldn't be visible through the doorway.

If the shooter came in the front and looked, even with infrared, he would not be able to see her body as long as she stayed low, so Pauling again belly crawled along the exterior of the building foundation, grateful there were no loose stones.

And then she was away from the building and into a stand of ice plants. Pauling got to her feet and began to run, hunched over, slowly, as she could barely see anything in front of her. Certainly nothing beyond arm's length.

Forward was the only thing she knew, away from the building and the shooter.

Her face hit stone and pain slapped her in the face. Pauling felt blood trickle from her nose into her mouth and the taste was both coppery and dusty.

She felt with her hands and eventually came to the edge of the structure. She leaned around, feeling foolish because she couldn't see anything anyway—

Cement exploded just above her head accompanied by the sound of a shot.

She turned again and ran. With no idea where she was going she raced at full speed. It was a terrifying run. All the shooter had to do was get around that building and if he had a night scope could easily put a round right between her shoulder blades. She tensed as she ran, waiting for the blow—

Suddenly, she was airborne and falling.

Too late, Pauling realized she'd run right over the edge of the cliff and something viciously struck her on the shoulder and she rolled. A stabbing pain pierced her side along the hip and she rolled again, bounced, felt branches scratch at her face and her knees scraped rock.

Finally, she came to a stop.

Her body screamed in agony, blood was wet on her face and she wondered how far she'd fallen.

If the sniper stayed on the edge with his night scope he would be able to pick her off easily. Pauling knew she needed to get under some sort of cover. And then she heard the faint sound of waves crashing and she instantly recognized her location.

She had stood at this very edge with Gabe and she remembered the large rock outcropping near the ocean.

Her mind raced back to that night with Gabe, which had been moonlit. Now, it was pitch black.

Pauling scrambled ahead, certain that any minute a bullet was going to crash into her and blow her body apart.

Her feet hit water and she remembered the crevice of

rock that opened up onto the beach, with deep ledges on either side.

The water was ice-cold but at least she wasn't visible. Pauling forced her way through the water and around the edge until she was under a little ledge. At least now she was out of the water and hidden, but she was cold and hurt.

Instinctively, Pauling appreciated that there was no way the sniper could get into the water and to her without making a sound.

No one was that good.

The thought of the shooter entering her sanctuary motivated her to feel around until she found a good, fist-sized rock.

If her attacker came into the water she would hear and clobber him on the head. Not the most sophisticated of strategies and with little chance of success, but it was all she could come up with.

Pauling waited, keeping her mouth open as cold began to seep through her bones so her teeth wouldn't chatter.

After several minutes she thought she heard something. The sound of a boot, maybe something hitting water and then she heard a soft laugh.

Pauling waited, but no one came after her. She lost track of time, put the rock down and folded her arms across her chest, trying to generate heat.

She was going to stay here until daylight.

If she didn't die of hypothermia first.

CHAPTER FORTY-SEVEN

B lake studied the requests Nathan had sent to the investigator's office regarding information on Paige's death. They had released some initial findings and documents but not the autopsy results even though Nathan had specifically requested that. It appeared the official response had been that the state of the remains prevented any meaningful findings.

But, like Pauling, Blake wondered if that meant they hadn't found anything at all. Had they tried?

Blake realized that hacking the server of law enforcement was not a great idea, even though he'd done it before. The challenge, naturally, was that law enforcement had the means to investigate hacks as a criminal violation. Companies had to first prove the hack on their own and then go to the authorities. Which was why hacking the authorities themselves was a much riskier proposition.

However, the email correspondence between Nathan and the clerical branch did give him a window.

It was much easier to hack into email than into confidential servers.

So that's what he set about to do. Using the main email address he was able to reach the email server and after several hours of digging, Blake located an email from one of the investigators to another investigator with an attachment. It appeared the attachment might contain information from Paige's autopsy.

Blake got in and was able to download the attachment. He then sent the full document to Pauling via his own encrypted system knowing full well that she was on an island controlled by the military who were no doubt monitoring electronic communications. Especially Pauling's.

He used a basic encryption code that he knew Pauling would understand right away and that would throw off at least a preliminary glance from anyone on San Clemente Island. It wouldn't stand up to serious scrutiny, but he hoped it would go through as is.

It did.

CHAPTER FORTY-EIGHT

Pauling never felt as cold and tired as she did the minute she woke up.

The sun had just started to peek into the crevice of rock where she had crawled, and the change in light had no doubt roused her.

She stretched her limbs and they audibly creaked. Her face felt stiff and her lip seemed puffy. She remembered running into a wall.

At least she was dry, although her feet still felt a little wet. Maybe that was why she was still so goddamned cold.

Pauling climbed down from the ledge and realized that she could walk to the left out onto another lower shelf of rock that led to part of the beach.

She started to walk out into the full sun but stopped. She peeked around the ledge first looking for any sign of a sniper or rifle and understood how foolish that was.

Those guys could be two feet in front of you and you would never know it. But still, she scanned the horizon and saw nothing so she stepped out into the full sun, grateful for the warm at the same time bracing herself for a shot that never came.

Pauling hiked along the water's edge until she found a trail that led back up the cliff. She scrambled her way up and got to the edge and saw she was a quarter mile down from Rag City.

She slowly worked her way around the rocky terrain until she came to the road and hoped there was a car but none appeared, so she walked on until she got back to the Nest. She opened the door, walked in and the first thing she heard was Janey who let out a little gasp.

"Oh my God!" Janey whispered. "Pauling! Are you okay?"

Pauling gave her a half-hearted thumbs up and walked past her, staggered back to her room and flopped on the bed, then rolled over and pulled the covers on top of her. She closed her eyes and within minutes was sound asleep.

She had another dream that took place in the desert. This time, a gunman was chasing her and in the distance, she could see Paige, waving to her. Pauling ran, but just when she was about to reach her, a bullet hit her in the back and she fell face down in the desert. Her mouth was filled with grit-

Pauling woke up, and her mouth was dry. She was sore all over and she briefly relived what had happened at Rag City. She remembered the shots, being chased and falling off the edge of the cliff.

Pauling got up, went into the bathroom and looked at her face. No wonder Janey had reacted the way she did. Pauling looked just like what she was. A woman who'd been chased, shot at and had taken a few major tumbles.

What a mess.

She had scratches on her face and when she lifted her shirt saw a bruise the size of a baseball on the side of her hip.

That's really what hurt the worst. But in retrospect, she was glad. If she'd landed on that rock just a little bit higher she would be looking at about three or four cracked ribs. Who knows, if she'd been really unlucky, maybe even a punctured lung.

And then she probably would've died out there.

Overall she was lucky.

It just didn't feel that way.

Pauling had met her fair share of Special Ops soldiers. When they took a shot, they rarely missed. She dabbed her cuts with a warm washcloth and soap, wincing in pain as she scraped the dried blood from each wound.

It was true, Special Ops guys were the best in the world. So why had the shooter missed? She thought about it. It was night. Pauling was running. Hiding. They wouldn't have been easy shots to make.

Another possibility arose in her mind.

Maybe the shooter hadn't wanted to kill her. Maybe his shots had gone exactly where he'd wanted them to. Near her. Just over her head.

They weren't intended to kill.

Maybe he'd just wanted to scare her.

When she was done cleaning herself she took a hot shower and got dressed. She took several Tylenol and washed them down with tap water. Immediately, Pauling felt a lot better. Still not one hundred percent, but seriously improved.

She thought about reporting the crime, but what would she say? The first question asked would be about what exactly she was doing in Rag City.

Would they really buy a mysterious message about a rendezvous?

Something told her the military guys wouldn't really care. They would chalk it up to a birdie making a big deal out of nothing. Probably scared by nearby gunfire that had nothing to do with her.

Pauling went out to the kitchen, thankful that no one was

there. She poured herself a big cup of lukewarm coffee and went back to her room. She opened up her laptop and checked her email.

Only one message.

From Blake.

Pauling opened the attachment and began to read the autopsy on Paige. There was the usual preliminary information but about halfway through the report, the examiner noted several marks that he couldn't attribute to shark bites.

He simply labeled them indeterminate.

She wasn't trained to read autopsies but it did seem to her that there were a lot of marks on Paige's body labeled as inconclusive. If Paige had truly drowned and all the damage been done by sharks, shouldn't every mark on her body be labeled as such?

Pauling made the immediate decision and she fired off multiple emails, one to Blake and another to Nathan's attorney stating in no uncertain terms that Paige's remains should be immediately exhumed and sent off to a pathologist she had worked with in Washington, DC.

He was retired now but he had been the best in the business. In the email to Nathan, Pauling stressed that he needed to move heaven and earth to get the remains exhumed immediately and overnighted to the pathologist. She wasn't satisfied with the autopsy.

And she knew Nathan wouldn't be either.

Pauling picked up the satellite phone and called Nathan.

"Pauling," he said when he answered.

"How secure is this line?" she asked. Pauling didn't want to waste a lot of time speaking in code.

"Fairly secure," he said. "But one can never be too careful."

She sighed. She then told him what had happened but avoided using names as much as possible.

"I never had any doubt," he said when she finished giving him the details.

"I know you didn't," Pauling replied. "I feel I'm still a long way from finding out exactly what happened, but what I do know is that we're a lot closer than we were a week ago."

"That's for damn sure," he said. "I knew you were the right person for the job. Call me the minute you hear from the examiner. Those inconclusive marks are going to be the key."

"Of course. We'll talk about Jack Reacher when I get back," she added.

"Have you been working with him?" he asked. His tone sounded very hollow.

"No," she replied. "No sign of him. In fact, no one's ever heard of him."

"Do you want other backup?" Nathan asked. "You've got snipers shooting at you for Christ's sake. What if I sent in another person undercover who could act as your bodyguard?"

She could tell by the tone of his voice that he knew it was a bad idea and that it was really a token offer.

"No, I'll just have to be more careful. Besides, if another new volunteer showed up here, I'm sure no one would do any more talking. Then it's a full-on, blatant investigation. At least now I've got some doubt on my side."

"You're right," he said. "Keep me posted."

They disconnected and Pauling thought about those inconclusive marks on Paige's body.

She wondered why the investigators hadn't been surprised by the autopsy results either.

Maybe they hadn't wanted to be.

CHAPTER FORTY-NINE

The next day Pauling checked the bulletin board to see who was working where in the field. She saw that Ted was operating in the south field, one of the few places she had yet to visit. Pauling put on her walking shoes, got a big bottled water from the fridge and set out. Her body was still stiff and sore, especially her hip, but walking under the sun she soon felt much better. Her face wasn't showing any lingering effects of its meeting with a cement wall.

It took her nearly an hour and a half of hard walking to get to the observation post.

Pauling wondered how she was going to handle Ted, since the last time they'd chatted he'd practically taken off her head.

She stood at the observation post, opened the box containing field notes, and began to flip through them. As she expected, they meant virtually nothing to her and she saw that Paige hadn't written anything.

Suddenly she heard voices coming from the trail and she assumed it was Gabe and Ted.

Ted emerged from the field first and behind him was a man as young as Ted but whom Pauling had never seen before.

Both men stopped in their tracks. Deer in the headlights. Pauling noticed Ted's hair was especially messy and the young man's shirt was pulled out of his jeans.

Before they'd spotted her they both had a relaxed happy look on their faces and Pauling knew instantly what they'd been doing.

Suddenly it all made sense to Pauling.

Ted's surprising anger with her over pursuing the investigation. He'd attacked her with vigor and now she

knew why.

He'd had a very dangerous secret to protect.

Pauling knew that homosexuals in the military were really not welcome. Officially, policies had begun to change but unofficially, gay men in the military was still an uncomfortable subject for a whole lot of people. While Ted wasn't in the armed services, it appeared his companion was. So Ted was no doubt protecting him.

"What you doing out here?" Ted said.

"I've never been out here before," Pauling answered, her voice relaxed and cheerful, as if she hadn't put two and two together. "I was curious to see this area and figured maybe I could help."

The young man stepped past Ted and wore an easy smile on his face. He stuck out his hand.

"I'm Jim," he said. Pauling shook hands with him and Jim turned to Ted.

"We should get back, he said. "I've got to start work in about a half hour."

Ted's gaze lingered on Pauling for a moment and then they walked past her.

She stood there in the sun, pretending to flip through the field notes.

Pauling waited the requisite amount of time to make sure Ted and his companion were well on their way and then she put everything back in place, turned and began the long walk back to the Nest.

This little island is just full of secrets, she thought.

CHAPTER FIFTY

Pauling had been right about Nathan, but in a way she had also been wrong.

He had, in fact, moved heaven and earth and probably spent a prodigious amount of money greasing the right hands. But it took him more than three days to get the remains exhumed and sent off to the medical examiner of her choice, Dr. Milton Killibrew.

Dr. Killibrew had been one of the most famous pathologists in all of law enforcement. Pauling had gotten to know him when she was at the FBI.

They had worked together on a particularly vicious case and Pauling and Dr. Killibrew had bonded. She had even gone to his retirement party where he'd said that if she ever needed any help he was always available for her. Pauling laughed as she remembered him saying that he didn't golf, fish or like the beach.

He just liked to work.

When the first message came through via email encrypted, Pauling opened up Dr. Killibrew's report.

It began with the usual disclaimer that this was just

preliminary and that he planned to spend at least several more days with various body parts under the microscope to get a better understanding.

Once she'd gotten past the obvious vital details, he confirmed shark bite marks and agreed that there were several wounds that were inconclusive. But it was the last thing on the report that caught Pauling's attention.

It had also obviously intrigued Dr. Killibrew.

The renowned pathologist described discovering a very small piece of lung that had been hidden in a mass of cartilage and bone. He stated that under the microscope it appeared to him that the level of salinity and oxygen could lead to only one basic conclusion.

Again he provided a bevy of disclaimers but in the end he said he would be willing to testify to a 95% certainty rate. The conclusion made Pauling sit back.

Paige had been dead before she went into the water.

CHAPTER FIFTY-ONE

Murder.

There was no other explanation.

Pauling sat back and thought about her next steps. The investigator's name was on the report. And it belonged to the Los Angeles County Sheriff's Department, but not the officer on Catalina Island. The report had been generated in Los Angeles proper.

She toyed with the idea of emailing or calling him, but then she quickly dismissed it. She knew she would get nowhere on the phone or online.

It was time for a different tactic. She thought it through and came up with a plan. She went to her things, dug through to the bottom where she had hidden Nathan's stash of money and peeled off three thousand dollars worth of bills.

Next, she commandeered a truck.

She drove up to the airport and waited for the plane from the mainland to come in. It arrived every day of the week except Wednesdays, Saturdays and Sundays. Its usual arrival time was early afternoon, but that could sometimes change depending on weather but with a clear sky and no sign of storms, Pauling was confident it would land at its regular time, in about a half hour.

She used the time to think.

If Dr. Killibrew's finding was true, it meant beyond almost all certainty that Paige had indeed been murdered.

There could be no other explanation for how she had been dead before she went into the water.

That would mean she hadn't drowned.

So if she had already been dead, how did she get in the water?

The easy answer was a boat. Somebody who had access to a boat most likely killed her, took her out into the middle of the ocean and dumped the body.

Of course, there were a lot of military guys who had access to the boats. And probably quite a few who used them even if they weren't authorized. So it was a pretty big pool of possibilities.

Still, there was only one person she knew who had both a boat, and a beautiful set of blue eyes.

Michael Tallon.

CHAPTER FIFTY-TWO

The plane landed and Pauling stood up. She went to the window and watched the half-dozen passengers disembark. They all appeared to be military personnel.

The engine gradually shut down and the pilot, Jamison, got off the plane but stood outside talking to some of the military guys.

The flight coordinator came into the building and went into the office just off the main room. Pauling remembered him from the bar when Deb had tried to pick a fight with her. She remembered his name was Troyer. Josh Troyer.

Pauling walked over to the doorway and looked at him. "Hey, when is the next flight out?" she asked

Troyer looked up at her. He shook his head. "That ain't how it works," he said.

"I know," Pauling said. "But I really have to get to Los Angeles as soon as possible."

The flight coordinator shook his head. "We're going later today but you know there's a two-week waiting list to get on the flight plus all of the paperwork. You're usually looking at almost a three-week wait before you can get on the plane. This isn't exactly Delta Airlines."

Pauling walked over to him and slid the bundle of cash out of her jacket and put it on the desk.

"Consider this an expedited rate," she said, "for a round trip."

Troyer looked at the money, then glanced over at the guys on the tarmac. Finally, his gaze returned and settled directly on Pauling.

He smiled.

"Good news," he said. "We just had a cancellation. There's now an open seat on the last flight out today."

Pauling glanced down and saw that the three grand had disappeared from the top of the desk. She smiled.

"What time do we board?"

CHAPTER FIFTY-THREE

The seats on the plane were empty, but the cargo hold was full. Pauling saw the boxes and crates, along with what looked to be some machine parts, packed into the hold at the rear of the plane.

Jamison waved at her from the fold-out stairs. She carried her pack and climbed into the plane.

"No comedy routine today," he told her. "Pick a seat. Any seat."

Pauling noted that the plane was completely empty.

She sat in the first seat across from the door opening and tossed her pack into the empty seat next to her.

"It'll be a quick flight," Jamison told her. He winked at her and she could tell from the expression on his face that Troyer had cut him in on the deal. He would have had to otherwise there would be no explanation.

Pauling was beyond excited to be back in the real world. She couldn't wait for her regular cell phone to work again. And she really wanted to spend the night in a hotel and sleep in a real bed. But that would all depend on what she found out.

They finished loading and Troyer climbed aboard. He nodded and grinned at Pauling, then went into the cockpit and closed the door.

The engines revved and very quickly they were airborne. Pauling looked out the window as San Clemente Island fell away beneath her.

The plane banked and she saw the rolling waves of the Pacific. A few minutes later, they passed over Bird Shit Rock and Pauling saw a large, dark shape a hundred yards from the outcropping of land.

A great white, for sure. She shivered involuntarily, thinking of her diving for lobster with Michael Tallon. She could've been a tasty snack for that shark.

The flight was short and the landing smooth.

Once on the ground, Pauling took a cab to the Los Angeles County Sheriff's Department, located in the Hall of Justice. Pauling briefly thought of some kind of superhero reference.

She went inside and found her way to the department in charge of accidental deaths. After all, that was what Paige's death had been ruled.

Ultimately, she found herself seated across from a tired-looking man with dark circles under his eyes and a neatly trimmed beard. He had a white shirt with a collar that was just starting to show signs of staining.

"Paige Jones, let me see," he said. His name was Gianfranco and he thumbed through a file cabinet looking for the name.

At last, he pulled out a folder and set it on the desk between them.

He flipped it open.

"Drowning," he said, "followed by shark feeding."

Gianfranco looked up at Pauling.

"So what are you investigating, exactly?" he asked.

"I don't think it was an accident."

He sat back in his chair and smiled at Pauling.

"I've got twenty detectives working overtime on a backlog of cases. Even with that, we look at every case. If there had been any indication foul play was involved, it wouldn't have wound up in that file cabinet. Trust me."

Pauling thought about what he'd said.

"Is there any other reason it would have wound up in that file cabinet?"

His big, dark eyes peered out at her.

"It seems like the investigation was not very thorough. Rushed, almost," Pauling said. "And when I spoke with one of your colleagues on Catalina Island, I felt like I was practically thrown out of his office."

Gianfranco gave her a tired smile. "You seem like a sharp lady," he said. "Can you think of any reason a cop on Catalina might handle a death on San Clemente a bit gingerly?"

"The military, of course," she answered. "If they were involved in limiting the investigation. But why would they care about Paige Jones drowning?"

"I'm sure they didn't care then and I'm sure as hell they don't care now."

"Wait a minute, you're not making any sense," Pauling said. "You're contradicting yourself."

"No, I'm not. What I'm saying is they probably didn't care any more or less about your relative's death. But they don't want anyone investigating anything out there. Do you know what I mean?"

Pauling did understand him.

"You've been out there, right?" he said.

"Yes."

"Then you know as well as I do there is a ton of clandestine shit going on. You've got FBI guys out there, CIA, Spec Ops. Who knows, maybe they've got a part of the island where they torture terrorists."

"I don't think so," Pauling said. "But the point is, they don't want anyone asking. At all. Period. So there must be some sort of unofficial standing order that if anything happens on San Clemente at all, the military will actually handle it and you guys take a back seat."

"I would deny that with my last dying breath," he said.

Maybe she had been wrong, she realized. Maybe there hadn't been any interference run on Paige's death specifically, but it was just standard operating procedure for anything that happened.

Gianfranco seemed to read her mind.

"That island is bad luck, though," he said.

"What do you mean?"

Gianfranco closed the folder and put it away before Pauling could sneak a glance at it.

"We had a girl a year ago come back here to L.A. from that island, get in a car and disappear. Never found again. She's a cold case now."

Pauling couldn't keep the awestruck expression from her face. How could no one else have known this?

"I want her name," she said.

"Why?"

"Because maybe she knew Paige," Pauling said, winging it. "Maybe looking into her background can help me put together a cohesive description of what happened, if nothing else."

Gianfranco eyed her warily, pulled the folder back out and said to her, "Donnellon. Emily."

He put the folder back in the cabinet, shut it and locked it and then scooped up his coffee cup in one smooth motion.

"I hope you're not forgetting what we just discussed," he said.

"Oh, I'm not."

"Great. I'll show you out," he said.

CHAPTER FIFTY-FOUR

Pauling put in a quick call to Blake and had him run the name Emily Donnellon, making sure she would get the right one. Pauling could have used some of her services back in her office in New York, but since Blake was free, she chose him.

He called her back within minutes.

"Good news," he said. "She lived in the Valley. Went to UCLA. Her parents still live in the family home, according to utility records, combined with her school records."

He gave Pauling the address.

She took a cab to a car rental company, rented a sedan and drove directly to the Donnellon family home, a split-level ranch with a GMC SUV in the driveway.

Pauling parked her car and knocked on the door.

A woman looked out, then unlatched the door.

"Can I help you?" she asked.

"Mrs. Donnellon?"

"Yes."

"My name is Lauren Pauling and I'm looking into the death of Paige Jones. She died on San Clemente Island. I understand your daughter Emily disappeared after returning home from the island?"

It all came out quickly but Pauling figured it was the best way to do it.

"Please, come in," the woman said.

She led the way to a living room. It was immaculate, with an upright piano against one wall, a seating area with a couch and chairs facing a gas fireplace.

Mrs. Donnellon sat in one of the chairs and Pauling sat across from her on the corner of the couch.

Pauling briefly studied the woman. She was probably in her late fifties or early sixties, with a stylish haircut and a trim body. She looked a little bit like a California beach bunny, all grown up and doing well.

"Do you think they're related?" the woman asked.

"I'm not sure, Mrs. Donnellon," Pauling said.

"Please. Call me Julia."

"Julia, I'm not sure because frankly I just found out about your daughter. I've spent the past couple of weeks on the island trying to find out what happened to Paige, and no one even mentioned it. Which surprises me."

Julia Donnellon shrugged her shoulders. "Maybe they don't know. Emily only spent a week out there and she landed here in Los Angeles. It was after that she disappeared."

"Did she come home? To this house?" Pauling asked.

"No. No one saw her."

"Who was the last to see her?"

"When the passengers disembarked they were all checked off at the airport. That was the last time anyone saw her."

"Were the police able to find anyone who picked her up? A friend? Did she call a cab? Taxi companies record most of their calls and obviously keep track of who picked up fares and where."

Julia Donnellon shook her head. "No, they contacted all

of the cab companies but no one could find evidence of picking her up."

"So she was last seen at the airport."

"Yes. They used her cell phone records to see that her phone was turned on when she landed. But then she didn't make any calls or send messages afterward. And then she disappeared and the phone was never used again."

"So she couldn't have called a friend or a cab, then?" Pauling asked.

"We figured she didn't have to call. Sometimes there are cabs just waiting at the airport to pick up a fare. That's probably what happened."

Pauling thought about the small, military airport with its secured gate. Not a place a cab driver would hang out looking for fares.

"Do you have a photo of your daughter I could look at?"

Julia Donnellon got up, left the room and came back with a photo in a frame.

Pauling looked at the girl in the picture. Blonde. Blue eyes. Very pretty.

Not exactly like Paige, but in the ballpark.

"Beautiful," Pauling said, and handed the photo back.

Mrs. Donnellon set the photo on the coffee table between them. Pauling felt like the girl was looking up at the both of them.

"Now what?" Julia asked.

Pauling stood. "Thank you for talking to me. I'm going to fly back to San Clemente Island and see if I can talk to some people who might have known both Paige and Emily. See if there is any kind of connection. Is there a phone number where I can reach you if I have any questions?"

The woman jotted down a number and gave it to Pauling.

"Good luck," Julia Donnellon said, her voice heavy with sorrow and fatigue.

"If you find out what happened to Paige, maybe you'll find Emily."

Pauling nodded.

She didn't have a good feeling about it, though.

CHAPTER FIFTY-FIVE

Pauling was never a big believer in coincidences. And something felt very wrong about the situation. Two beautiful girls, one dead and one missing?

It just didn't add up.

How was it no one on San Clemente Island felt the need to mention that Paige wasn't the only young woman to have possibly been harmed?

Was it that they didn't know?

Or were they trying to hide it?

Obviously, it wouldn't play well for the reputation of the Bird Conservatory to have young women continually experience harm while working for them. Or, in this case, just after.

Nor would it be good for the military people on the island. There was certainly a fraternity there of men who protected their own.

It wouldn't be the first time a group of men had covered up crimes against women to protect their own.

Pauling mulled all of this over as she returned the rental car and took a cab to the little airport. She noted that there were no cabs waiting to pick up fares.

There was no excitement over the idea of going back to San Clemente Island, but now Pauling had a whole new set of questions to ask. There was a surge of adrenaline, though, at the prospect of confronting Dr. Sirrine, Wilkins, and even Michael Tallon.

Had Tallon known Emily Donnellon?

If he was all about seducing beautiful women, Emily would have fit the bill. She had been a breathtakingly beautiful young woman.

Pauling also wasn't looking forward to going back under what they call the cone of silence. A lack of Internet and lack of cell phone coverage was conducive to a feeling of disconnectedness. Even though she had the satellite phone and could communicate with Blake via email, a sense of isolation was pervasive on the island.

Pauling made her way to the old airplane and walked up to Troyer, who was overseeing the loading of more cargo.

He turned to her. "There she is," he said. "Our lone passenger."

She took her seat as they finished loading the plane. Once her gear had been stowed, Pauling sat down and pulled out her phone. It might be the last time she had quick and easy access to her email.

She checked her mailboxes and saw a message from Dr. Killibrew. Attached was a Word document with a more thorough analysis of Paige's autopsy.

The plane hurtled down the runway and then lurched into the air. Pauling momentarily put her phone down to hold onto the arms of her seat. It was windy, and the old plane creaked and groaned as it gained altitude.

Once it was calmer, she got the phone back out and opened the document.

The fourth paragraph made her gasp out loud. It stated:

... S ubject appears to have suffered from a full body concussion initially misdiagnosed as blunt force trauma. A more accurate diagnosis with a higher degree of accuracy would state that the trauma was consistent with suicide jumpers...

T he phone dangled in Pauling's hand.

Suddenly it made sense.

When Paige had been placed into the ocean she had already been dead.

But what she suddenly realized was that Paige hadn't been tossed into the water from a boat.

She'd been dropped from somewhere much higher.

And no one had seen Emily Donnellon once she'd gotten off the plane.

Pauling knew why: she'd probably never gotten off the plane in the first place.

At least not on land.

The realization sunk in and then she felt the cold, razor-sharp edge of steel placed against her throat.

"Whatcha reading there, honey?" the voice asked.

CHAPTER FIFTY-SIX

"I was reading all about your handiwork," she answered through gritted teeth.

"Yeah, how so?" Troyer asked.

He stayed behind her.

"Pretty slick," Pauling said. "Find your victims, get them on the plane alone, have your fun, then dump them into the ocean. More specifically, a part of the ocean full of hungry great white sharks."

She heard him chuckle.

"Lean forward and put one arm behind your back," he said.

Pauling had no choice but to comply.

"It was you at Rag City, wasn't it?" Pauling asked.

"Yeah, we get bored when we have to overnight on the island."

From the cockpit, Jamison appeared. He smiled back at them, and he had a small pistol in his hand.

"It's a .22," he said, reading her mind. "I can shoot you, but it won't go through the fuselage. The perfect caliber for this sort of thing."

Pauling felt the knife removed from her throat, and then cold steel snapped around her left wrist. The snap of the handcuffs closing seemed to echo in the airplane.

"She was asking about our fun shooting at her in Rag City," Troyer said.

"I'm a helluva shot," Jamison said. "Missing you was easy but I tried to get as close as possible. For the effect."

"How'd you put the note under my door without being seen?" Pauling asked.

"Easy. The Nest is empty all the time. That's how we searched your room, too."

"Put your other hand behind your back," Troyer said.

"Whoo boy, I've been waiting for this ever since we flew you out here," Jamison said.

"That's pretty pathetic," she said. "Can't compete with the military guys, huh? 'Cuz they're young and athletic and you're middle-aged and soft?"

She wanted to piss them off, get them to momentarily forget their cool, and she desperately wanted at least one hand free.

However, she knew methodical killers rarely made mistakes. It was when they were distracted that they failed to think things through.

Jamison slapped her.

It was a quick hard move and it rocked her head back. She tasted blood.

Troyer used the slap to grab her arm and snap the cuff on it.

Pauling spit the blood out at him. "What a great idea," she said. "Kill them on the plane. No witnesses. Plenty of time to get rid of evidence. Hell, you could even doctor the flight records to make it look like they landed in Los Angeles."

"Oh, they landed all right, just not on terra firma," Troyer said. His voice sounded cool and collected. Jamison still looked flushed, pissed off at what she'd said.

"Can't they track your flight records?" Pauling asked, stalling for time. "I'm assuming you put the plane on autopilot while you have your fun?"

"Oh, we just divert due to weather for awhile. No big deal," Troyer answered.

"Yeah, you look like you'd be pretty quick in the sack," Pauling said, meeting Jamison's eyes. "Little-dicked buddies spurned by women, right?"

Something snapped in Jamison's eyes and he slid the pistol into his pants and lunged at Pauling.

She lowered her head and butted him in the sternum, then spun and grabbed for the pistol with her hands behind her back. Jamison grabbed her and they tumbled together onto the floor.

Pauling was lucky. She landed on top of the gun and was able to get ahold of it. However, she was pinned on top of it and couldn't budge it, so she squeezed the trigger.

The sound was an explosion and Jamison screamed. Troyer jumped off of her and she lurched forward, getting the gun out of Jamison's pocket and she aimed it blindly behind her and down. She pulled the trigger multiple times and then spun as Troyer reacted.

He came at her but she shot. The bullet went high, catching him in the throat. He stopped, and then staggered. Pauling lowered the pistol and fired two more times until the hammer clicked on empty.

Troyer fell, the front of his shirt a bloody mess.

Pauling looked down, behind her, and saw that one of the bullets she'd fired into Jamison had gone in under his chin and come back out through his left eye.

They were both dead.

Even worse, the plane was tilting down and Pauling had a

moment to wonder if one of the bullets had gone into some wiring or fuel lines.

She looked to the cockpit and saw through the windshield a sky of blue.

Except there was a wave in the sky.

And then she realized the blue wasn't the sky, and the wave was real.

The plane crashed into the ocean and Pauling's world went black.

CHAPTER FIFTY-SEVEN

C old.

Pauling's world went from black to cold. And then to bright white. Foam filled the airplane as it creaked and heaved in the cold ocean water.

Her hands still locked behind her, she struggled to her feet. The crash landing had snapped a wing off and taken a chunk of the fuselage with it. The sun burst through the opening, along with a steady roar of ocean water.

Suddenly, the sun was gone, replaced by a glow as the plane sank beneath the surface of the water. Pauling instinctively dove toward the opening, unable to use her arms, instead, kicking with everything she had. She made it through the opening just as the plane heaved to the right. She felt something stab her left leg and then she was kicking upward.

Her head broke through the surface and she gasped, taking in a huge lungful of water.

She bobbed under, then back up. She rolled to her side and then to the other.

To her right, she had glimpsed the top of Bird Shit Rock.

She rotated her body and rolled onto her back, and began kicking furiously.

Her leg was burning and she had the sickening realization that she was probably bleeding.

Not a good thing with sharks everywhere.

Pauling was tempted to try to stop and confirm if she was bleeding, but what would be the point? She continued to kick and twist to remain on her back.

She was sure at any moment something huge would crunch through her legs.

It took her an agonizingly long five minutes to reach the outskirts of Bird Shit Rock.

In those last few seconds she was absolutely positive something was going to bite off her legs.

But it never did.

She heard the waves splashing on rock and maneuvered herself into an opening between two jagged thumbs of rock. She could barely keep her head up to see, and each time the sea rewarded her by smashing her face with a vicious wave.

Pauling choked on the ocean water but crabbed sideways, getting her feet beneath her and working her way around until she could stand and climb higher onto the outcropping.

She was safe, out of the water, but she was bleeding. The back of her leg was crimson and blood had seeped down, covering her foot.

Pauling wondered how long she would have to wait. The sun felt good on her skin as she shivered and closed her eyes.

CHAPTER FIFTY-EIGHT

"How long were you out there?"

Pauling looked up at Nathan.

"A couple of hours," she said. "The military air traffic control guys saw the plane disappear. They sent a helicopter out and they found me."

"You were lucky," he said.

"I know."

He sighed.

They were in a hospital room in Los Angeles, flown directly there by the search and rescue team. She'd had a mild concussion and some bruised ribs. The jagged cut on her leg had taken twenty-seven stitches.

In a few hours she would be released and able to head back to Wisconsin on Nathan's private jet.

Not that she was all that anxious to get back on an airplane.

"You did it," he said.

"A lot of luck was involved," Pauling said.

"Those bastards got what they deserved," Nathan said. In

some ways, he looked more tired and older than when she'd last seen him. But there was something different in his eyes, too. A sense of closure, maybe.

Justice.

"There may be more than Paige and Emily," Nathan said. "The cops are scouring their files for any other missing women. They think they've already found one."

Pauling knew they would. Jamison and Troyer had gotten very good at what they were doing. And they'd gotten that good through practice.

Plenty of practice.

"I owe you an apology," Nathan said. "I'm sorry about using the Jack Reacher story to get you to take the case. I had read about your background and knew you were the perfect person to find out who killed Paige."

Pauling let it go. She wasn't happy about it, and she'd almost died, but she wasn't going to tear into Nathan Jones now.

There was movement in the doorway and Pauling saw Michael Tallon looking at her. He had a clutch of flowers in his hand.

"Well, I'll see how soon we can get you out of here," Nathan said. He nodded at Tallon as he left the room.

"You know if you'd wanted to see Bird Shit Rock up close all you had to do was ask," Tallon said. He gave Pauling a sheepish smile and put the flowers on a table at the foot of the bed.

"Pretty impressive, what you did," Tallon said.

"Thanks," Pauling answered.

"How long was I a suspect?" he asked, with a twinkle in his eye.

"Not very long," she answered.

"Before you trusted me," he said.

"Who said I trust you?"

"You don't?" he made a big deal of looking shocked. "What do I have to do to earn it?"

She glanced out the window and then looked back at him.

"I've got a few ideas in mind."

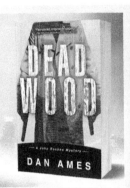

ABOUT THE AUTHOR

Dan Ames is a USA TODAY Bestselling Author and winner of the Independent Book Award for Crime Fiction.

www.authordanames.com
dan@authordanames.com

ALSO BY DAN AMES

The JACK REACHER Cases #1 (A Hard Man To Forget)
The JACK REACHER Cases #2 (The Right Man For Revenge)
The JACK REACHER Cases #3 (A Man Made For Killing)

DEAD WOOD (John Rockne Mystery #1)
HARD ROCK (John Rockne Mystery #2)
COLD JADE (John Rockne Mystery #3)
LONG SHOT (John Rockne Mystery #4)
EASY PREY (John Rockne Mystery #5)
BODY BLOW (John Rockne Mystery #6)

THE KILLING LEAGUE (Wallace Mack Thriller #1)
THE MURDER STORE (Wallace Mack Thriller #2)
FINDERS KILLERS (Wallace Mack Thriller #3)

DEATH BY SARCASM (Mary Cooper Mystery #1)
MURDER WITH SARCASTIC INTENT (Mary Cooper Mystery #2)
GROSS SARCASTIC HOMICIDE (Mary Cooper Mystery #3)

KILLER GROOVE (Rockne & Cooper Mystery #1)

BEER MONEY (Burr Ashland Mystery #1)

THE CIRCUIT RIDER (Circuit Rider #1)

KILLER'S DRAW (Circuit Rider #2)

TO FIND A MOUNTAIN (A WWII Thriller)

STANDALONE THRILLERS:

THE RECRUITER

KILLING THE RAT

HEAD SHOT

THE BUTCHER

BOX SETS:

AMES TO KILL

GROSSE POINTE PULP

GROSSE POINTE PULP 2

TOTAL SARCASM

WALLACE MACK THRILLER COLLECTION

SHORT STORIES:

THE GARBAGE COLLECTOR

BULLET RIVER

SCHOOL GIRL

HANGING CURVE

SCALE OF JUSTICE

Made in the USA
Monee, IL
29 March 2022

93749276R00125